T0067093

The
APPRENTICE BOY
— *Part II* —
CAPTURED FOR BURIAL RITUAL

LUKE OKOLI

authorHOUSE®

AuthorHouse™
1663 Liberty Drive
Bloomington, IN 47403
www.authorhouse.com
Phone: 1 (800) 839-8640

*This book is a work of fiction. People, events, places and
situations are the product of author's imagination.*

Published by AuthorHouse   03/18/2015

ISBN: 978-1-4969-6453-3 (sc)
ISBN: 978-1-4969-6452-6 (e)

Print information available on the last page.

This book is printed on acid-free paper.

*I am dedicating this book to my
wife and my children.*

If you have read Part 1 of the APPRENTICE BOY,
the synopsis below will assist you to recapitulate
and reconnect with the trend of the story while
you read Part 2. (If you have not read Part I,
you will still enjoy the book fully). Read on:-

Ike was a Nigerian boy who loved to go to school but
had nobody to help him. He did menial jobs for people
inorder to raise money to pay his school fees. He was
not always successful in making money for his school
requirements and for maintaining the family. He was able
to take the Standard Six First School Leaving Certificate
(FSLC) Examination only because a kind pupil lent
him the money to pay his school fees for the final term.

Although Ike was a very brilliant student, he could not
attend the secondary school education despite the fact that
he had a wealthy uncle. Ike's father died as a result of a fall
from the palm tree. His mother took ill a few years after
and became paralyzed. Ike and his younger brother Emeka,
four an two years respectively, started from that tender
age to cater for themselves and their bedridden mother.

Because he had nobody to support him in school, Ike later
went to learn a trading business with his uncle at Onitsha.
He did marvelously well in the course of his apprenticeship.
But his interest remained to go to school. Through self-
effort, Ike read at home and got his GCE certificate.

When Ike was about to complete his apprenticeship at Onitsha, an incident occurred which punctured his career. He returned to the village to start life all over. In one of his usual fishing expeditions, Ike fished in a prohibited syndicate fishing pond of the Nzom natives. This was a deadly mistake. He was captured and taken away by the brutal Nzom murderers who did not spare anybody that trespassed their fishing ponds.

CHAPTER 1

When Emeka got home that evening after escaping from the hands of the Nzom fishermen, he couldn't go into the house to relate what had happened to his mother. He was afraid that his mother might ask him about Ike.

Enmeshed in confusion, Emeka trembled with fear. His breathing kept coming in short rapid bouts. Time without number he asked himself if this was a dream or a reality. His whole being was shattered as he began to think of returning to Okuiyi Ngene to find Ike. But he lacked the guts to venture back into that deadly zone. He feared that what happened to his brother might happen to him too. He wrestled with two options – to go back to Okuiyi Ngene, or to go into the house and relate the tragedy to his mother. Hiding behind the house he cried quietly. No one knew he was there.

He had been crying since he escaped from the people who took his brother. He was shaking with fear and did not know how to tell his mother that Ike was killed by the Nzom fishermen.

Adaego was unaware of what was going on behind her house. She knew that her children, Ike and Emeka, went to fish as usual, but had not returned. She wasn't comfortable. Intuitively, she felt that something had happened that had delayed the boys.

They have never stayed this long, she thought as she assembled the ingredients for the dinner. What are they doing? It's getting dark. Is everything well with my children? she wondered. Did they meet some mishap? Were they drowned in the river? But they can swim very well. In any case, does it matter who can swim and who cannot? I have seen experienced swimmers drowned.

Adaego kept turning these probabilities over in her heart. Every now and then, she peeped through the window to observe the position of the sun. She estimated it would be five o'clock in the evening, yet her children were not home. The boys usually returned before noon. What are they doing? she kept asking herself. She became worried but kept hoping that they would soon come in to tell her what had been holding them. She picked up her cane and struggled to the door.

From outside, Emeka heard some movement within. He thought that his mother would soon discover he was outside. He was in a big dilemma - go in and break the sad news or rush back to Nzom in search of Ike? He needed to make a decision before his mother appeared at the door. On hearing the click of the door, he dodged behind the orange tree. From there, he disappeared. He did not know how to begin to tell his mother that he lost Ike at the hands of the Nzom guards.

"I can't," he said to himself in tears and hastened off.

He decided to go back to Okuiyi Ngene to look for Ike dead or alive. I must go to look for him, he thought, even if it means my death. What is life without Ike? How on earth can I tell this story? Oh, Ike, my brother. Where are you? Are you dead or alive? Ike, can you hear me? Tell me where you are. I want to meet you, even if you're dead. I want to rescue you. Are you wounded somewhere? Oh, can the gods hear me? Can my ancestors hear me? Oh, my only companion in the world. How can I live without him? What does life mean without Ike? Never! I must find him, dead or alive. Either I find him or what happened to him will happen to me too.

He increased his speed. It was getting late in the evening. The shadows were elongated, stretching to a breaking point. Soon the sun would sink into the horizon and darkness would envelope the atmosphere, it would be too dangerous then to set foot on Okuiyi Ngene.

Signs of dusk were around. The purple stain of twilight was deepening rapidly; domestic animals were homebound; hens with their chicks were foraging close by the houses picking their last morsels before retiring to their roosts; the birds shuffled in the tree foliage vying for sleeping places.

Market women, with baskets on their heads, hurried home to prepare dinner for their children. Exhausted farmers walked home feebly with their hoes hanging on their shoulders.

Suddenly an idea came to Emeka and he decided to branch off to collect some people to accompany him back to Nzom.

The first man he stopped to see was Ike's friend, Nnamdi. Nnamdi and Ike were the best of friends during their elementary school days. They played together. They fished together. Sometimes they went to the bush to hunt rodents or to collect firewood. They went to the river to swim. Even though they had left school long ago, they were still good friends.

When Emeka arrived at his house, Nnamdi was whetting his hunting knife in preparation for a hunting expedition tonight. He was a hunter. Once or twice a week he went to the forest with his friend, Ifediegwu, to hunt wild games. Nnamdi had a dane-gun which he inherited from his father.

Like Ike, Nnamdi had no opportunity to go to secondary school after his primary education. So he became a farmer. He combined both farming and hunting. In rural life, there was hardly any clear-cut demarcation on what people do for a living. For example, a carpenter can be a farmer too. A fisherman can be a bricklayer, a farmer, a petty trader, and a watchnight.

"Emeka!" Nnamdi greeted him gleefully as he approached. "It's been a long time since I have seen you. How is my friend, Ike? And how is your mother?"

While he was speaking, tears rolled down Emeka's eyes. Nnamdi was taken aback. He knew that something was wrong. He dropped his knife and held Emeka by the hand.

"What's wrong? Is everything okay? What happened? Tell me," Nnamdi asked in quick succession.

Emeka was sobbing profusely. He couldn't talk. Nnamdi knew that this must be a serious matter. He wiped his hands on his waist cloth and took the young man inside his house. He began to ask Emeka what had happened and why he was crying. Amidst sobs, Emeka narrated the incident to Nnamdi.

"Oh, Good Lord!" Nnamdi cried and stared above the roof. "This is a bad story. Ike shouldn't have gone to Okuiyi Ngene to fish. The Nzom people are brutal. They are wild. Did they catch him?"

"I don't know," Emeka replied, still crying, "but since he is not home yet, they might have caught him. When they came after us we took to different directions. I ran into the bush and escaped. I assumed Ike did the same. When I got to the coast, I waited, but he did not appear. And when I got home, he wasn't home either."

"Oh no, God forbid! I hope they didn't catch him. Nzom people are animals. They kill at sight. Oh, I wish my friend escaped from these devils. But he may have run off course to a distant farm-land, and wandered away. He might be alive."

"If he is alive, where is he?" Emeka asked in frustration. "This thing happened during the morning hours. If he missed his track, he could've found his way home by now."

"Did you say in the morning hours?"

"Yes, in the morning."

"Let's go," Nnamdi said and picked up his gun and his machete. "Let's go and search for him. I can't leave my friend to perish like this. We'll see the end. Let's go."

Before they headed for Okuiyi Ngene, they stopped at the houses of a few young men and collected them. These men were equally as hefty as Nnamdi, full of energy and vibrating with youthful vigor. They set off for Okuiyi.

When they got there, the sun had gone down. Without wasting time, Nnamdi and his men began the search for Ike. Emeka showed them where they were fishing when the Nzom guards struck. He explained how the men emerged from ambush and closed up on them. He pointed at the direction where he made his escape and showed them the direction Ike headed.

The search party combed the bushes and shrubs. The objective was to find Ike dead or alive. They didn't find anything.

Holding his gun in a combat position, Nnamdi led his men around the scene of the incident. They were all armed in case the Nzom guards reappeared. They searched the whole place, but neither Ike nor his body was found.

Wandering further, they came to a spot where they saw blood-stains on the leaves. They followed the trail and saw more blood-stains. The men concluded in their mind that the Nzom fishermen had killed Ike.

Seeing what he believed to be his brother's blood Emeka began to cry. There was no doubt in his mind that the blood on the grass was Ike's blood. He believed they had killed him. He released a deafening scream that tore through the evening tranquility. His voice re-echoing from the distance hills:

"Ewooooo! Ewooooo! Ike my brother is gone, Ewooooo! Ewooooo! This is his blood! He is dead! How can I tell the story? I went to fish with my brother, and this is the end result. Oooh, my only brother! Oooh,

Ike, where are you? Are you living or dead? Ewooooo! Ewooooo!"

The men tried to appease him but he went wild with wailing,
"Ewooooo! Ewooooo! Ewooooo!
Ike, come out of your hiding place,
Ifite men with their clubs and mace
Are here, your rescue is sure,
Come out, you're secure.
"Ewooooo! Ewooooo! Ewooooo!"

Nnamdi looked up above and shook his head. Tears dropped from his eyes. "Oh, something has happened," he moaned and concealed the tears for that was a sign of weakness.

It was getting dark. The men were exhausted. They couldn't find Ike nor recover his body. They called off the search and returned home.

CHAPTER 2

Already, news about Ike's disappearance had spread at Ifite. Almost everybody, except Adaego, had heard what happened. Nobody told her. The neighbours stood on their toes looking over the fence to see if she had heard what happened.

Sitting in her house in total confusion, Adaego was sure that something was amiss. Never had her children stayed out this late. She was restless. Occasionally she dragged herself to the door to ask children returning from the river whether they had seen Ike and Emeka. Earlier, she had sent a message to Nkiliuwa, one of her neighbours, to tell her what was going on.

"Tell Nkiliuwa that *the snake is in the fibers,*" Adaego told a small girl. But Nkiliuwa was not home. She always came back late from the market.

Adaego continued to look down the road leading to the river hoping that her children would soon return. They did not.

Shortly after, the search party, led by Nnamdi arrived at Adaego's house. Two elder men, Ozee and Egbuna, accompanied them. Nnamdi and his men had branched off to collect the elders to help explain the situation to Adaego. Elder statesmen know how to reconstruct a sad story to cushion off the agonizing impact it will have on the victim.

Seeing the visitors, Adaego yelled out in a stentorian pitch, believing that her children were dead. "Where are my children?! Oh God, where are my children? Are they dead?"

Emeka shoved his way to the front of the crowd to show he was alive. His mother grabbed him and hugged him.

"Where's your brother? Where's Ikechukwu? Where is he? What happened? Is he dead? Where...? Ewooooo! Ewooooo! Ewooooo!" she wept.

"Emeka tell me what happened."

The men were looking. Emeka did not speak.

"Where's your brother? Can somebody tell me what happened to Ike?" She screamed at the top of her voice. They tried to appease her but she would not stop wailing and screaming. She had no doubt in her mind that Ike was dead.

Emeka began to cry too. This lent credence to Adaego's suspicion that Ike had died. She threw herself down crying and weeping. She kept calling Ikechukwu's name, asking all the people she knew, dead and alive, to tell her where her son was and what had happened to him. The drama went for a long time and it seemed the people could not control the situation.

The neighbours heard Adaego's voice and began to drop in one by one. They watched mother and son weeping and reeling in anguish. They assumed that Ike had been killed by the Nzom fishermen.

After a while, one of the elders spoke, "Woman, calm down and listen to me."

But Adaego would not stop. "I want to know what happened to Ikechukwu my son," she wailed. "Let someone tell me where Ikechukwu is. Is he dead? If he is dead, please tell me. Oh my God! Oh my world! Ike! Ike! Ike! Ikechukwu my son! Ikechukwuooooo! Ikechukwuooooo! Oh, heavens! *After seeing this, eyes will go blind.* This is the end of the road. I'm finished."

Adaego ignored the man who was trying to calm her. She went on wailing.

"Ike my son is gone, Ike my son is dead. I'm finished. I'm dead. What am I living for? I'm finally finished. I'm done with life. Oh, God help me. Take me, Oh God. What does my life mean now? Why should this happen to me? What have I done? My son is gone. I know he's dead. Can somebody tell me what happened to him? Was he killed? Was he drowned? Emeka what happened to your brother? You too can't tell me? Where's your brother? Where is his body?"

Her voice stirred families throughout the neighbourhood. Most of them had gone to bed. Adaego's house was full with sympathizers. Seeing that Emeka was also crying, nobody was left in doubt that Ike was dead. Adaego could not be appeased.

"If you don't want to calm down and hear us," one of the elders said in frustration, "we shall leave this place,

11

and then you can cry all you want. We have been trying to calm you down to discuss the matter, but you prefer to cry without knowing what you are crying for. Who told you that Ike was dead? You don't even know what happened, yet you're..."

"It's my son, Ike, he's dead," Adaego cried.

"Who killed him?" the elder asked her reproachfully, "you?"

Adaego's voice mellowed down after the man had spoken irritably. "Oh, my son Ike, where are you?"

Some women weaved through the crowd and began to console her. "Adaego, we understand your situation," said one of them, "but hold on for a moment and let's hear what the elders want to say. It's not yet clear what happened to Ike. No one has confirmed that he is dead. Close your mouth and let's hear what these men have to say."

"That's right, let's hear what the men want to say," another woman agreed. "It's not clear yet what happened to Ike. Some people are saying he is alive. Close your mouth."

Adaego didn't stop crying but she lowered her voice, humming like stirred bees.

When there was calm, one of the men said, "We're in your house because the Nzom guards attacked our sons Ike and Emeka, who went to their fishing pond. Emeka managed to escape, he's right here with us. But no one knows what happened to Ike. We hope he escaped too. His brother said the Nzom guards took them by surprise."

Amidst the speaker's speech, Adaego yelled out like a psychotic patient who was experiencing an episodic bout.

"Owners of the fishing ponds often keep watch over their property," the speaker continued. "They wait in an ambush and, at the spur of the moment, attack the trespasser. They attacked Emeka and Ike, and the boys ran to different directions.

"It's too early to say they killed Ike. He may have run astray into a distant land in an effort to escape from the assailants. We assume that he is alive and will return home, right, men?"

"Right," they agreed in one voice.

"Tomorrow, more people will go to the pond to continue the search. Tonight, I'll detail Mbamalu, the town-crier, to summon able bodied men of Ifite for the search. Hopefully Ike will come back to us. We shall try our best to find him. Stop crying our daughter."

With that last statement, the elder tapped the end of his cane on the floor and headed for the door.

CHAPTER 3

That same night, the town crier went around the village summoning the ablebodied men to appear at the village square in the morning.

At dawn, the village square was filled to capacity. All the men in the village were present. At the middle of the discussion, a seasoned village head, Ibezim Iloanya, warned Ifite people to avoid hostility. He explained: "The sole objective of this mission to Nzom is to search for our son, Ike. If we find him or his body, we retrieve it. The intention is not to attack anybody, unless we are attacked. We are not going there to fight," he emphasized, looking at the direction of the youth. "I have heard some people clamoring for war. What justification do we have to attack Nzom? The question is, why did these boys fish in their pond? The pond is a private property. Those of you who clamour for war should be reminded that Ifite does not fight a blame-worthy war. That's why we have never lost any war in history."

There were murmurs of disapproval in the crowd after Iloanya had spoken. "Coward!" said a young man.

A challenge came from Chief Ezenekwe Ofieli. The young men liked Chief Ofieli because, even though he was an elderly man, his actions depicted the radical characteristics of the youth. He was more militant and aggressive in his approach to issues than other older folks.

Addressing the gathering, Chief Ofieli told his people that Ifite could no longer endure the humiliations of Nzom. "The excesses of these murderers must be checked," he stressed. "Last year, they murdered our son, Ikebudu Nwokolo. The year before, they had killed Anigbogu, six months ago, they killed a fisherman from Ozida village. And this year, they killed our son, Ikechukwu Anierobi. Why should we sit here folding our hands? Why should we watch them erase us from the face of the earth? I'm not a party to this female talk. Let's send our young men to Okuiyi Ngene to teach Nzom people a bitter lesson. It's high time we cut Nzom's tail which is growing too long for our comfort."

The meeting split into two groups after Ofieli's speech. One group favoured immediate attack, the other group supported noncombatant approach, at least for now. This group proposed that Ifite should send emissaries to Nzom to look for the missing young man. If they did not find Ike or his body, they should ask the Nzom people questions. Nzom's response would determine their next line of action.

This opinion received the majority approval. The idea of going to war was, temporarily, shelved.

One of the most respected members of the clan, Nwako Obidigbo, summarized the purpose of the mission to Nzom,

"Your mission to Nzom is to look for Ikechukwu, no more. If you find him, bring him home, dead or alive. If not, the elders will meet again to decide what to do next."

CHAPTER 4

At Port Harcourt where she was working, Nneka received the sad news about Ike's misfortune. She was devastated. She became ill without any symptom.

As the story spread, people twisted and changed the contents. Nneka had heard many versions of it. Some people said Ikechukwu was hacked to death at Okuiyi Ngene. Others said he was kidnapped. Another version said he got drowned in the river. Yet another source said a hunter mistook him for a game and shot him to death. Different versions of the story came from different people who traveled to Ifite over the weekend.

A source said Ike might be alive because his body was not recovered by the searching parties. This compounded issues for Nneka who was anxious to know what happened to the only man she loved in the world.

One thing was clear; Ikechukwu Anierobi was missing and could not be found. Nneka feared that Ike might have been killed, for she heard that the men who went to look for him saw traces of blood at the scene. This piece of information was evidentially crucial to the version of the story which held that Ike might have been killed.

The sad news hit Nneka so badly that she became depressed. In her office, she could not function. She sat moping in one direction, to the point that if somebody entered her office, she would not know. She was miserable and downcast. Her boss advised her to take some days off. Everybody in her office had heard what happened, and they sympathized with her.

Ike was the only true friend and lover Nneka had in her life. He was her future hope. Since she came to Port Harcourt, not a single day passed without her thinking about Ike and dreaming about him. She had had uncountable nightmares as well as some lovely dreams about Ike. Often she kept herself busy constructing a glorious mental edifice of her future life with Ike. She often imagined how fun and satisfying it would be to stay with him for the rest of her life.

When men proposed to her, she did not entertain their courtship. She could never forget the evening when Ike proposed to her. She recalled how Ike held her hand while they were taking an evening walk. Her heart melted when she remembered that first kiss under a tree in the twilight.

The sad news made Nneka change her lifestyle. These days, she could hardly eat food. She began to look emaciated and unkempt. She bottled up herself in the house and ignored everybody and everything. She often asked herself, whether this story was real or just a dream?

Nneka believed she had gone through a lot of mental anguish because of Ike. She had just recovered from the previous incident - Ike's affair with Angela at Onitsha, his subsequent dismissal from work, and now this. She wondered what type of ill-luck she had, and the type of checkered life Ike had.

Nneka planned immediately to go to the village to verify what was going on. Without waiting to obtain a permit from her work, she left for Ifite.

On the bus, she was thinking:

If Ike was at Onitsha doing his business, this would not have happened. His carelessness brought about these woes. This is a chain reaction of his misconduct at Onitsha. I didn't expect Ike would disappoint me in my life. I never knew Ike would change. I thought he was cultured, quiet, and responsible. Now see all that is happening around him. He has ruined his life and mine too.

Oh, Ike has destroyed my heart, she wept. Now who knows if he is dead or alive? Oh! Ike, my beloved. Are you dead or alive? Where are you? I don't want anything to happen to you. Please stay alive for me. I need you, despite your mistakes. I still love and cherish you. Don't die. I can't bring myself to believe that anything will happen to you. You must not die. God, he must not die, please. Protect him for me.

Before Nneka knew it, she was already at the Ifite motor park. She was buried in deep thoughts and did not know when the two-hour journey was over. On arriving in her village, she went straight to Ike's house, without first stopping at her home.

When Adaego saw Nneka, she burst out crying louder. She had been crying all day and her voice was hoarse. Nneka threw herself on the floor and wept bitterly.

Both she and Adaego plunged into a spate of weeping and wailing. Visitors and sympathizers who were in the house watched them. They wondered who the beautiful girl was. One of the women whispered to another,

"She is Ike's future wife."

"Really?"

"Yes. She's the daughter of Helen Akigwe."

"Oh, Akigwe the bricklayer?"

"That's correct."

"So Helen has got a grown girl like this?"

"Yes. And she is very beautiful."

"I can see it. I don't know her."

"She's not at home," explained one of the women, a neighbour." She's working at Port."

"Really? I didn't know that Helen has a big girl like this."

"The present generation grows like poultry chicken."

"I know. What's her name?" one of the women with a protruding tooth asked.

"Nneka," replied another.

"Is this that Helen's skinny little child who used to pass through my compound with her bucket of water a few years ago?"

"Exactly. She's the one," agreed the neighbour.

"I think she was the one that was stung by a scorpion in my garden years back?" another woman said pensively.

"That's right," the neighbour agreed. "You know her very well. You have a good memory Mama Nku. I'm surprised you can still remember that little incident that took place years ago. You might as well remember the very words your husband spoke to you the first day you went to his house for the traditional eight-day home-study."

The women laughed.

"You are silly Iyom," Mama Nku replied to the neighbour. "What about you, you never told us why you stayed twenty days with your new suitor instead of the customary eight-day home-study period. Tell us what you were doing."

The women burst into suppressed laughter covering their mouths. They had to hide their temporary lighter mood disposition because this occasion did not call for expression of lighter but sombre temperament.

Days passed and nothing changed. Ike did not return. Sympathizers were still pouring into Adaego's home to comfort her. Emeka was sitting at a corner, hands folded across his chest. He was at a complete loss. Since the incident, he and his mother did nothing but cry. They couldn't console each other. They didn't cook or eat anything. They could not even eat the meals neighbours and relatives brought over.

Some close relatives stayed temporarily with them offering support. Adaego's sister, Ifeatu, had been with them for a week. She brought large quantity of food which the visitors ate. She took charge of the house. She cooked, served, fetched water, and cleaned up.

Also, Nwosu Anierobi, the elder brother of Ufele, was there, receiving guests who came to grieve with Adaego. Nwosu, in his late sixties, was the person Adaego liked and respected in the Anierobi family. He was a benign, cultivated, and peaceful man. Unlike his brother Ufele,

Nwosu was open-handed and very supportive of his late brother's family. Although a poor man, he always tried to assist Adaego in any way he could. Adaego wished that Nwosu was the rich one in the Anierobi family and not Ufele.

Many members of Adaego's extended family were in her house on condolence. Acquaintances and friends across the village came by to verify the news they heard about Ike.

In Igbo culture, bereavement is shared. Families that suffer a loss are not left to grieve alone. Other family members, neighbours, and friends, are always around to render emotional and material support. This support system had existed among the people for ages and is still effective today.

CHAPTER 5

The following day, Nneka and Adaego were still crying. Their eyes were red.

"Is there any hope of recovering Ike?" Nneka asked Adaego listlessly, her voice cracked.

"Recovering who?' Adaego asked dismally. "Recovering a dead person? How do you do that?"

"Nne, don't say that," Nneka rebutted. "Ike is alive."

"What makes you think that my son is alive? Has anyone ever fallen in the hands of Nzom people and come out alive? My son is dead!"

She burst out again and wept.

"In my mind," Nneka declared, wiping her own eyes, "something is telling me that Ike isn't dead."

Adaego regarded Nneka in a jejune manner for her childish reasoning. "What are you talking about? He is dead. I can't believe anything less. They are only trying to deceive me. I know that my son is not a living person. If he is alive, where is he? Twice the Ifite men had gone to Okuiyi ponds to search for him; twice they found nothing. And you are telling me that Ike is alive. What kind of story is that?"

Again, she began to cry.

"It's most likely that they killed and dumped his body into the river, "Adaego said amidst sob. "I know he's not alive. Oh Ike, Ike my son! Oooooooooh! I am finished."

Both of them went into another spate of lamentation.

Nneka turned to Emeka who was sitting at a corner, "Emeka how exactly did it happen?" she asked.

Emeka was depressed and totally down in the dumps. Within these few days, he had lost weight. His eyes were sunken and he had begun to emaciate. His tears had dried up and he couldn't cry anymore but brooding and glooming.

Although Nneka had heard bits and pieces of what happened, she wanted to hear from the horse's mouth. She leaned her back to the wall with her hands folded on her chest.

Emeka gave her a detailed account of their ill-fated fishing expedition. He left nothing out. As he did, Nneka poured out tears sequentially.

He also told Nneka that they went to the fortune-tellers to find out whether Ike was alive or dead.

Nneka's feelings were assuaged on hearing that a renowned seer at Ihube disclosed that Ike was alive somewhere.

"The fortune teller told us that she could not locate Ike's spirit among the dead," Emeka said, "which means he is not dead. Also, Ike's age grade went to the house of Ifediegwu, the famous sorcerer at Ulasi, to find out what happened to my brother. Ifediegwu told them that she saw three men chasing two young men with knives and spear."

"And what happened next?" Nneka asked impatiently.

"The sorcerer said the gods did not see the spirits of the men and they would not reveal further details to her."

"Does it mean that the unrevealed aspect of the findings is grim?" asked Nneka.

"I… I… don't…"

"All these stories are empty chronicles," Adaego interjected pessimistically. "They are nothing but unveritable instruments of fortune telling business. Seers have to tell you what you would like to hear so you can pay them for their services."

"Nne, Ulasi does not charge fees for her services," Emeka argued.

"Who said so?"

"She doesn't. She merely accepts donations."

"There you are. Whether you call it a fee, gift, or donation, they mean the same thing – means of livelihood. Fortune tellers make their living through these means."

Outside the house under the shade of the tree where the men were drinking palm-wine, the same debate was going on: Do seers actually see *things?* For example, can they see things that the ordinary eyes cannot see? Can they invoke dead people? Do seers communicate with spirits, and can we take their words and predictions seriously?

Already some old men had started mooting about Ike's funeral. They were talking among themselves that Ike was not a living person and that his burial should begin. Others believed that more time should be allowed.

Some cultures in Igboland do not perform the funeral of a missing person. Men who suddenly disappeared in a community, or who were lost in tribal wars, were not given immediate burial.

CHAPTER 6

"What do you plan to do after weaning this child?" Nnedi asked her grand daughter, Angela. "You know that in a few months Ikechukwu will be two years old, at which time you are supposed to stop breast-feeding him. By then, you will be free to go wherever you want to go, and the child will stay with me. What plans do you have and what do you intend to do?"

Angela stared at her grandmother reflectively scratching her head. She searched her mind for a reply, but nothing was readily available. It never crossed her mind to think about what she would end up doing when her baby became older.

Being a single mother and nursing a fatherless child is not an acceptable part of Igbo culture. To start with, people frown at young girls who had babies outside marriage. They are disrespected. Suitors sidetrack them because they believe that the disgraceful behaviour will continue even when such girls are married. In their opinion, the stigma lives with such women for a long time. Today, however, it's not much of a taboo to see a young unmarried woman with a child.

Angela's condition made her miserable because, like the bat, *she did not belong to the airborne creatures nor the land animals.* She was not a girl neither was she a married woman. Sometimes she was ashamed of herself and ashamed of her low self-esteem. She often regretted that mistake of sleeping with a man, and wished it had not happened.

This situation notwithstanding, Angela truly loved her baby. That was her consolation in life. Anytime she was overwhelmed with sadness, she would coddle her baby and would derive solace from the child. A great bond existed between her and the child. His presence had become a vital instrument for strengthening her broken spirit.

Nnedi's question had put Angela in a difficult situation. "Nne," she said, shifting her stool closer to her grandmother. "I have not really thought about this question. What do you want me to do?"

"Every mature person has his or her life to lead and his or her life's goal to pursue," Nnedi replied. "You are old enough to decide what you want to do. As an old woman, what I like may not be what you like. Besides, these days, young people prefer to do their thing their own way. We're the older generation. Our thoughts and opinions no longer hold sway for the youth. In the past, parents influenced their children's decisions. Today things have changed. Therefore you should know what is best for you."

Nnedi knew why she said this, but Angela did not.

"Nne...I...I know I'm mature to handle my affairs, but... I would like you to deliberate with me. They say *two heads are better than one.* Do you have anything in mind?"

"What about getting married?" Nnedi suggested and watched Angela's reaction. That's what the woman had been nursing in her mind. She wanted Angela to get married and begin to raise her own family since she had started it a little too early.

Angela's face contoured. She shifted her stool backwards, a sign of rejection. She gazed balefully at Nnedi with probing eyes. "Getting married you say?"

"Yes, getting married." the old woman repeated. "What's wrong with that?"

Angela stared at the dog that lay beside her. The dog was half asleep and half awake, flapping its ears repeatedly to ward off the menacing flies that were attacking a tiny wound at the tip of its ear.

Angela's face was ashen revealing disappointment. Her grandmother's response wasn't close to what she expected to hear. The issue of marriage never crossed her mind. After her ordeal with Ike at Onitsha, talking to her about men or marriage infuriated her. She hated men now.

"I... How can I... Nne do you mean getting married to a man?"

"Do people marry dogs or goats?" Nnedi asked humourously.

They laughed.

"Does it sound strange to you? Yes, I mean to get married to a man, that's exactly what I mean. You're a woman, you can't get married to a woman, or to a tree, or to something else. I mean to get married to a man and raise a family of your own."

At this point, the conversation drifted from its warm beginning to something disconcerting. Nnedi noticed a little resentment in her granddaughter's face, something she seldom saw. Her statement was unsavory to Angela. Angela summoned courage and retaliated repugnantly,

"Nne, should I go from door-to-door asking men to marry me? Is it customary?"

Nnedi backpedaled, "My daughter, don't misunderstand me. As you rightly pointed out, it's not customary to go from door-to-door looking for a husband. Women do not go out seeking men, at least not in our culture. I'm not saying you should take wine to a man to make a proposal. It's not done. What I am saying is that you should begin to think about getting married, especially now that you have had one child. In as much as I do not intend to coerce you into something you are not ready for, I want you to begin to think about this matter."

"Are you then suggesting I should display myself, like a commodity, for sale?" Angela retorted and moved her stool one more step backwards from her grandmother.

"Listen young woman," Nnedi replied in a hard tone. "I'm not asking you to go knocking on people's doors in search of a husband. What I am saying is this: a young woman who is nursing an idea about getting married, should have her eyes wide open with a view to identifying a suitor she might be interested in."

"But I'm not nursing the idea of getting married."

"You need to start."

"That's wrong," Angela shouted angrily. Immediately, she realized she had done the wrong thing. She must not raise her voice while talking to her grandmother who had been so nice to her, Nnedi could get upset by such a misdemeanor.

Nnedi loved her grandchild so much. Since Angela came to her house after running away from her parents, both of them were like *dung and beetle, or salt and oil,* inseparable. So she did not want to hurt Nnedi's feelings.

That's ridiculous! Angela said in her mind. Who ever told this woman that I was looking for a husband? I just can't understand why this topic came up.

"At their teen age," Nnedi began, "young girls rebuff talks about marriage. Topics pertaining to husband and wife, are inauspicious, they hurt too. However, at a later age, if a woman is still single, the issue becomes critical, and if she is unlucky to find a man, she's extremely worried.

"Now, what I'm trying to say is this, considering your present situation, you are not very marketable. I am not trying to offend you. I'm your grandmother, I can't deceive you. It's difficult for a woman in your situation to get married. I must be sincere with you. People believe that girls who defiled themselves and got pregnant in their parent's houses are not likely to make excellent housewives. As a result, men sidetrack such women believing that they will continue their waywardness if they married them. Therefore, your chances are not as bright as other girls. And the earlier you begin to think about this, the better."

CHAPTER 7

Angela was really hurt by all the things her grandmother had said about her condition. She interpreted Nnedi's statement to mean that she was a secondhand material which no man would want. She wished it were her mother or some younger fellow that said these things, she would've given the individual a rough side of her mouth. But she dared not talk to this elderly woman in a disrespectful way.

In Igbo community, older people are respected, whether they are male or female, right or wrong. So Angela swallowed her bitterness. She didn't want to hurt Nnedi's feelings. She thought she must choose her words carefully in talking to her.

"Then what do you want me to do in order to get married?" she asked her grandmother feeling helpless. Her voice was beckoning for help. She picked up her stool and moved closer to Nnedi.

"That's a good question," Nnedi said and adjusted her seat. "Good behaviour, good conduct, especially in the public place, that's the key. For instance, if a man talks to you, be courteous, humble, and respectful. Be friendly, polite, and obedient in your behaviour. Show humility; demonstrate the qualities of a girl capable of running a home; a girl who can be a submissive housewife; display good manners and show some interest." Do not rebuff or snub a ma...

"Nne, suppose he's a man I don't like?" Angela interrupted, "would I still need to adhere to all these rituals?"

"Good. You still have to portray polite behaviour, even if it's mechanically contrived. If you present despicable manners, they can spread bad news about your lack of good behavior. Don't forget that suitors ask questions about the woman they want to marry. That's the reason why you should always watch your behaviour no matter who talks to you. It never pays to be discourteous to people. Do you follow what I'm saying?"

Angela nodded her head, but in her heart, she didn't relish her grandmother's courtship 101 lesson.

Nonsense! Angela lashed in her mind, *these are all the obligations Ogidi must fulfill inorder to celebrate Nwafor festival?* These enslaving etiquettes are applicable in your days, certainly not today. I can't lick men's boots in order to get married. If I don't like a man, I will not marry him, period! If they don't want me because I had a baby outside marriage, that's fine. I have absolutely nothing to do with someone I don't like.

The thought about getting married wasn't in Angela's agenda, at least for now. She was discussing it only because her grandmother brought it up. She had no man in her life. Since her past affair with Ike, she had never talked to any man, and it didn't bother her.

"Nne, I have nobody in mind," she said and screwed her face.

"What about Odunze?" Nnedi suggested.

Angela threw her eyes wide open. She was rattled. "Which Odunze?"

"The one that frequents here."

"Odunze Iloegbunam?"

"Yes."

For a moment Angela was speechless. Then she found her tongue and guffawed loudly, "Ooooh, grandmother! This is the worst thing I ever heard in my life. You've ruined my day."

"Have I?"

Angela was distraught. She tried a short cynical chuckle which portrayed her disgruntled feelings. She clapped her hands in denial and spread them above contemptuously. Inside her, she was burning with irritation. She wished that Nnedi was a much younger person, or at least another woman, she would've opened a floodgate of verbal assault on her. But she swallowed her displeasure again.

She glowered at her grandmother and shifted her stool away from her. "That oaf of a man? That useless waif? Nne, do you really want me to have anything to do with that imbecile? I'm disappointed. I realize that I cannot rely on your judgment in assessing something of value. *I wouldn't seek your opinion or ask you to evaluate an article of purchase for me.* What do you want me to do with Odunze?"

"Did you call him a fool?" Nnedi asked.

"He is more than a fool. He is a useless nerd. Nne, do you know Odunze very well? I'm not sure you know him. Does Odunze know his right from his left-hand?"

"What makes you think so?" Nnedi asked irrelevantly as she picked up her snuff bottle and began to gauge its content. "What makes you think that a handsome man like Odunze is a nonstarter?"

"Odunze is a loafer, a good-for-nothing man, a busker... how can you recommend him to me?"

"It's a suggestion," Nnedi began to retrace her steps. "I didn't say you must marry Odunze. I simply made a suggestion."

"I know, but even at that, how can you advise me to consider him. What makes you think that I'd like to get involved with that idiot?"

Angela was fuming. Again she moved her stool farther away from her grandmother in protest. Each time she got angry she moved her seat away. And each time the conversation mellowed down to some degree of warmth she moved closer to Nnedi.

"Before you slaughter Odunze or me," Nnedi pleaded solemnly, "let me say a few things. This man hails from a very responsible and opulent family. His background is excellent. That's what matters. Odunze's father is a reputable man in this village. Who does not know Iloegunam? Every *rat and lizard* knows Odunze's father. Most people who are wealthy are stingy and tight-fisted, but Iloegbunam is very generous. His wealth is for the poor and the needy."

"Nne, these attributes are excellent," Angela told her grandmother clearly, "however, they are about

Iloegbunam. I'm yet to hear a single attestation about Odunze who is the focal point here, not his father."

"One man's wealth is as good as poverty," Nnedi continued, ignoring Angela's intelligent remarks. "One man's wealth does not impress anyone because he does not share. Chief Iloegbunam is a rich man and he shares. He has many economic trees. He has land, he has abundant resources. He has three wives. He has many children and Odunze is one of them. His children are responsible and progressive. Have you seen his new palm-oil industry at "Four-Corners?"

Nnedi waited for Angela to respond, but Angela didn't show any interest. Instead, she made another move to shift away from Nnedi, but this time she hit the wall having run out of space. She stared listlessly at the elderly woman. She was loaded with hate, not for her grandmother, but for this conversation and for Odunze in particular. She had no regards for the man who her grandmother was recommending.

"Odunze's father owns that oil mill known throughout Aguata," Nnedi went on. "Iloegbunam and his family are the most decent family one can think of in this village. I have known him since childhood. Never mind that he's rich now and relates to people of his class, I knew this man when he was going naked as a child. We played together as children in the neighbourhood. But he is now rich. Any woman who is married to that family is in good hands and will lack nothing. How come you have a negative attitude about them?"

"Nne, try to understand me. I have nothing against Chief Iloegbunam nor any member of his family. That's not the issue."

"Then what's the issue?" Nnedi asked brusquely.

"The issue is that I have no regards for Odunze as an individual. I don't like him. You've been busy explaining the good things about his father. Yes, Chief Iloegbunam is rich and has made a name, what about his son Odunze as an individual? That's the main point, that's what I want to hear. Who is Odunze? What is he among his peers? What has he achieved? What kind of person is he? These are the qualities one would like to hear, not Iloegbunam's wealth, fame, generosity, size of household, or number of wives and children. Has Odunze got any of this litany of assets, tell me?"

Nnedi reflected for a moment. She seemed to read some sense into what Angela was saying. Her argument holds water, she thought.

"You know Odunze better than I do," the woman said in capitulation, "what do you want me to tell you about him? Besides, I'm not basically trying to rope you into marrying him. I made the recommendation based on my casual observations."

"What are your observations?" Angela muttered glumly.

"I see Odunze here very often and I thought something was going on between..."

"Between who and who?" Angela snapped and rose from her stool.

She was hurt. She wanted to storm away and leave her grandmother to herself, she had had enough. But she changed her mind. Her head was whirling with indignation. The old woman knew she was fuming following that last comment. Then she said,

"I guess Odunze doesn't come here to visit an old woman like me, does he?"

"Neither does he come here to look for me!" Angela shouted. "I have absolutely nothing to do with that riffraff. Mama you've been very unfair to me, take note. Do you really think that I have something going on with that crook who stole his father's money last year and eloped with a whore?"

"What did you say?" Nnedi asked.

"Didn't you hear me? Odunze stole his father's *ten bags of money* and ran away to Otuocha with a woman. That's the man you want your grandchild to marry. Are you sure you love me, Nne?"

Angela's eyes were crystallized with tears. She turned her face away from Nnedi.

"Hmmm! I love you my daughter." Nnedi sighed with a sense of guilt.

"Do you notice that the man smells funny?" Angela asked her grandmother looking her straight in the eye. "Odunze stinks. He is also a drunkard. That's the person you are advising me to consider. Sometimes I begin to wonder how much you care for me."

Angela's voice changed. Tears began to roll down her eyes. Nnedi saw her emotion and became remorseful.

"My daughter, I love you and I care for you. I believe you know this."

"Then why would you recommend someone like Odunze to me? I have nothing to do with this man. He merely comes here to chatter like a charlatan. He is an asinine individual – a drunkard?"

"I never heard that." Nnedi confessed, as she wiped Angela's tears with the loose end of her wrapper. "Stop crying my daughter. I'm not betrothing you to Odunze. I never heard he steals. But his father is a very nice man. Well, that's the irony of life. *The womb that **bore** heroes also **bore** villains and hooligans.* Stop crying. I love you."

"It seems you don't even know the person you're talking about," Angela said amidst sob. "He is a miscreant. He raped an old woman a few months ago; he swindled a large sum of money from a neighbour recently; just last week, he was seen chasing someone's goat. That's the person you are proposing to me. Did you know that his father disowned him? Any way, let's cut a long story short, I don't want to marry, period!"

Nnedi glowered at Angela. "What did you say?"

"Did I have water in my mouth when I spoke? I said I don't want to marry."

"What then do you want to do with yourself young woman?"

CHAPTER 8

Angela looked at her grandmother thoughtlessly, and then looked at her child lying asleep on the floor. She hissed. She undid her wrapper and wiped her eyes and turned her face away from Nnedi mumbling something. The old lady looked at her repentantly and said,

"I know you're not happy Angie."

"I'm tired of this talk," she snarled grumpily, directing her anger to no one in particular. "I'm tired of life. I hate this world," she began to cry again.

"All of us do hate life sometimes," Nnedi said instructively. She sensed frustration. "Sometimes we feel indifferent about life. But we have to live because we are in the world. You're in the world my daughter, and you're still living. For everyone who is alive, life is not always easy. Who said it is?"

The woman looked at her grand child with unfeigned empathy and affection. "You don't have to feel too disgusted about everything," She said sententiously. "I can understand your frustration, but you are not the worst person on earth. If you go out there, you'll see people who have heavier burdens. Yet they go about their business. You're not the first person that made a mistake in life. Why should you hate your life because you became pregnant and had a baby? Forget the past and think about the future."

"But Grand-Ma, what you have said has exasperated my situation instead of making it better." Angela declared ruefully.

"I only made a suggestion," Nnedi said defensively. I am not betrothing you to Odunze, I'm not your father. I'm only making a suggestion. *If I used a male goat to make a reference, have I asked the lion to snatch it*?" If I suggested Odunze to you, did I say you must marry Odunze?"

Angela summed up the figure of speech. She believed that her grandmother was only making a suggestion and not that she wanted her to marry a man she did not like. She was appeased. She left her stool and sat on the mat where her child lay sleeping. She looked at him intently. A surge of good feelings ran through her heart. She stroked Ikechukwu tenderly and covered him properly with a piece of her grandmother's old wrapper.

She leaned forward resting her chin on Nnedi's lap in a warm and affectionate resignation. Nnedi began to stroke her head in a loving and conciliatory frame of mind. She saw that Angela was disheartened about what she had said concerning marriage. She thought that Angela's anger might not be directed to her in particular. It might be a dismal feeling, occasioned by her condition. She was concerned that her comments had shredded what was left of Angela's self-esteem. She regretted whatever blightful statements she had unwittingly made during their conversation. That notwithstanding, Nnedi insisted she could not compromise her obligations to guide her granddaughter to the right path. She patted her on the back affectionately and made her feel loved.

Nnedi wanted to change the topic. She wanted to ask Angela what she'd prefer to cook tonight. But before she did so, Angela said,

"Nne, I want to go back to school. I want to finish my studies."

"You want to go back to school?"

"Yes. When I finish my secondary school, I want to be a nurse."

"A nurse?"

"Yes."

"Like those who work in the hospital?" Nnedi asked.

"Exactly. Nne, how did you know that nurses work in the hospital?"

"I'm not that illiterate. Even though I didn't go to school, I know that nurses work in the hospital, you might as well ask me where the doctors work. Well, if you are interested in nursing, it's good. It's a nice work. Nurses are kind people. They are the most humble and refined people I know. They are very sympathetic and humane.

"I remember, years ago, before your father was born, I was sick and was taken to the hospital. The nurses took good care of me. I still remember this particular nurse who was very kind to me. She attended to me so nicely that people thought we were related We were about the same age. I'll never forget her. After that experience, I swore that one of my children must be a nurse. But unfortunately none of my children took to that noble profession. However..."

"Nne, tell me," Angela interrupted with curiosity. "What happened to you, why were you taken to the hospital?"

They were now talking more amiably. The tense atmosphere had dissolved. A friendlier air superseded. Angela turned and rested both arms on Nnedi's knees like a three-year-old, fixing her eyes on Nnedi's mouth solicitously.

Angela loved to listen to her grandmother tell her stories of the past, especially those stories that racked up information about the family tree - their ancestors' pattern of life; their beliefs, custom, and tradition. An avid listener, while listening to a tale, Angela would not move, not even when a millipede was crawling into her space. She could forego meals listening to Nnedi's stories.

"Tell me why you were taken to the hospital at that time when herbs were used to cure illnesses. Why couldn't the native doctors help you?"

"Herbs are still used today," Nnedi corrected her. "They are efficacious. Our native medicine is still powerful and very effective. Don't listen to the White man who says that our medicine is not good. They are ignorant of our culture. The only problem is that we don't know how to apply our medications more effectively..."

"More scientifically," Angela reframed the sentence.

"I went to the hospital because of child birth." Nnedi began.

Angela adjusted herself fixing her eyes on her grandmother's mouth. She stretched her long legs under Nnedi's stool and listened with rapt attention.

"There was this child birth problem inherent in my maternal lineage. My mother had the problem during her pregnancy years, and my grandmother had it too. Some of their daughters and sisters had it along the line. And many of them died as a result. My grandmother died of that birth disorder..."

"How did your grandmother die?" Angela asked impatiently.

"Which story do you want to hear," Nnedi asked. "Is it my own account, or that of my grandmother?"

"Let's go with yours first," Angela said and chuckled. She could trade all her money for a story.

"We have spent the whole day chatting," Nnedi remarked with concern. "Are we going to eat story tonight?"

"Nne, there's plenty of time. The sun is still bright. I'll be fast in the kitchen as soon as we are done with the stories."

"I do not relish late supper, Nnedi reminded her granddaughter. "Anyway, I had this childbirth problem during my third pregnancy. After the nine months gestation period, the baby would not come out. I waited for another three weeks, the baby would not come. Early one morning, after the tenth month, the labour began. The pain was unbearable. I couldn't deliver the baby. From the first cock-crow when the labour started till dusk, nothing happened. I was in a severe pain. I cried all day. I ate nothing because I had no appetite."

Angela looked at her grandmother sympathetically. She wanted to cry. She had experienced labour pains so she knew what her grandmother was talking about.

"Everything was done to bring out the baby, but it would not come out. I started bleeding profusely. I became weak and nauseatic. My body began to shake. I was dizzy, lethargic, and spasmodic. At this point, I feared I was going to die. I remembered my grandmother and I knew that what happened to her was happening to me. Death stared me in the face.

"Fortunately, Igwilo Ekediuba, my husband's friend, came to our house and met us in this awful situation. He asked my husband what he was thinking, seeing that this woman was dying. Throwing his hands up in despair, my husband said he did not know what to do. Ekediuba suggested taking me to the hospital. My husband agreed.

"Ekediuba ran home and grabbed his bicycle, and we left for Adazi hospital. My husband later told me that I passed out on our way to the hospital. He said they were three men on the journey, and that two of them suggested that the trip should be called off and that they should return home with my corpse. But my husband insisted they should continue to the hospital perchance the baby might be saved..."

"Oh my God!" Angela cried.

"My husband told me that when they got to the hospital, the doctors and the nurses battled hard to save the baby in my womb. Nobody was talking about me because they assumed I was dead. However, the doctors suddenly felt my pulse and began to revive me, and I came back to life. My husband believed that I hadn't gone too far to the land of the dead."

"Heeeiii!" Angela cried gleefully wiping her eyes. She hugged her grandmother empathically.

"I didn't know when these things were happening," the old lady said. "My husband gave me the account of all that transpired. He said the doctors cut my stomach open and retrieved the baby, and it was alive."

"Who among your children was this problem child?" Angela asked

"Your father."

To confirm her story, Nnedi pushed down her waist cloth exposing her wrinkled belly. "This is the operation scare," she explained to Angela, pointing at the faint marks of the surgery line. "I nearly died."

"Oooooh Grandma, you really suffered," Angela lamented running a finger across the stitches. "You bore all this pain?"

"Yes, I did. It was awful."

CHAPTER 9

"Now tell me about your grandmother," Angela said eagerly. She adjusted her sitting position obsessively ready for the next session of the family legend.

"Angela, shall we not eat tonight? It's getting late. I ask again, shall we eat story tonight? Is it not time to cook?"

"I'm not hungry," Angela laughed.

"I am," Nnedi said. "If you are not hungry, I am."

"Nne, after this, we will go to the kitchen," she coaxed the old woman.

Nnedi stared at her for a few seconds and then began,

"Well, in the case of my grandmother, her childbirth problem started exactly as mine. She was pregnant with twins. Her stomach was overstretched. Her pregnancy passed the normal gestation period of nine months and dragged into the eleventh month.

"Jesus!" Angela exclaimed. "Eleven months?"

"Yes, eleven months, and still nothing happened. At the twelfth month, the child labour began with increasing pain, yet she couldn't deliver the babies. Back in those

51

days, there were very few hospitals, few doctors, and few nurses. Women deliver their babies in their backyards with the support of other women."

"I thought there were local midwives who assisted women in labour?" Angela asked thoughtfully.

"Yes, we had such people, and we still have them today. But sometimes they are not available during an emergency. The local midwives are very successful in assisting women in labour, even in the most complex cases such as my grandmother's. Egodi was one of the rare women skilled in child-delivery art. But on that fateful day, she was on call to a distant village. From time to time, she traveled to different places to take care of complicated childbirth problems.

"Don't forget that at that time there was no transportation as there is today. People traveled several miles on foot. Motor cars were not available. The fastest means of transportation was bicycle which only few people could afford. Women did not ride bicycles then. Some distant journeys were accomplished in two or more days.

"Now, as I was saying, my grandmother's labour went on for days. Her pain increased day by day and reached a peak when the child started coming out the wrong way, one leg first. The rest of its body would not come out. That was exactly what happened to me in my own case. My child emerged with legs instead of head.

"As the labour struggle went on, my grandmother's strength began to wane. Behind the house where she was having the baby, some women were with her. They barricaded the scene with old sheet of mats. There wasn't much they could do because they were all inexperienced in the art of midwifery. Men were not allowed to come close the barricade. They came only at the behest of women to bring one thing or the other."

Angela was enthralled by her grandmother's story which sounded like a myth, but it was a true story of child-delivery experiences during the dark days. People who lived at that time saw the gruesome side of complicated childbirths.

"My grandmother went through a horrid pain," Nnedi continued. "The women who were at her side testified that she suffered a harrowing childbirth pains that no woman had suffered before."

Empathic tears crystallized Angela's eyes as she listened to her grandmother. Nevertheless, she was anxious to hear the whole story.

"My grandmother *saw her ears with her eyes,*" Nnedi went on. As she cried in pain, she voiced the following words in agonizing song:"

'Amagu Amaotu, what is amiss?
What have I done to deserve this?
Do women carry pregnancy for this long?
Amagu Amaotu, what have I done wrong?
In this land, Amaotu, I'm not a visitor.
Why am I cursed by the ancestors?
Fathers, are you asleep in your graves?
Hear my voice, I want to be saved?
This is my twelfth month of pregnancy.
Has invoking the gods lost its potency?
My ancestors, I ask, what is my sin?

I did what women do, both kith and kin
My fathers, isn't it normal to have a child?
Why should mine turn sorrowful and wild?
My Fathers, why should this happen?
Make haste, and have my pain dampen.
Amagu Amaotu, what have I done wrong?
Hear my cry, listen to my sorrowful song
I didn't steal from any man or woman,
I did not elope with any man or woman,
I contracted marriage the normal way
And my dowry paid on the appointed day,
I'm your daughter, blameless and innocent
I ask: Is this torment with your consent?
I've been suffering, I can't hold any further
Listen to my sorrowing voice, my fathers,
Amagu Amaotu, are the gods not awake?
Do they not have anything here at stake?
Death is lurking, I'm drowning in fear
Descend and wipe my agonizing tears…'

"Those were the words of my grandmother while she was dying in pain," Nnedi concluded. "She said so many things which people did not remember. Unfortunately the gods and the ancestors did not respond, and she died."

"Did she die?" Angela shouted in frustration.

"Yes, she died in that unfinished childbirth. Who wouldn't?"

"Oh, poor woman," Angela lamented amidst tears. "Where is God?"

"Before Egodi, the native midwife, could arrive, my grandmother had lost more blood than she had in her body, and she couldn't hold any longer. Egodi couldn't revive her. However, she was able to salvage one of the twins, and that one was my mother."

"Ooooh, this is painful indeed," Angela cried wiping her eyes.

"Yes it is painful," Nnedi agreed. "A lot of women suffered horrifying childbirth problems in those days and many of them died. Women suffer a lot, do you know that?" she said studying the contents of her snuff bottle. "You've experienced a little bit of it, there's no point explaining the pains of child birth to you."

"I'll not marry," Angela said again in resignation.

The old woman ignored her comment believing it was silly and childish.

"Now I have forgotten what brought us to this pastime." Nnedi said reflectively as she snuffed. "My memory is beginning to wane, old age. It's worsening day-by-day. I can't remember a thing any more. I'll soon forget my name too."

"You were talking about a nurse you met in a hospital," Angela helped her, "and I asked you what took you to the hospital? You also said you wanted one of your children to be a nurse."

"Thank you my child, that's where I was. Problematic childbirth was the reason why I went to the hospital. I couldn't deliver my baby.

CHAPTER 10

"Now, if nursing is what you want to do," Nnedi said wiping her nose, "it's good. It is a noble profession. I have no objection whatsoever. Have you told your father this?"

Angela hesitated, "No."

"Then tell him about it the next time you visit Onitsha."

Angela did not respond. She did not foresee any prospect in this suggestion. Her relationship with her father had gone down the hills. She visited Onitsha occasionally to receive her child support allowance. She hated to go to Onitsha because people in the yard looked at her boorishly. She had asked her father to be sending the money to her in the village. Jacob, knowing the reason, insisted she must come to Onitsha to get it, or else she'd starve.

Angela used to be her father's best child. Today, that affectionate relationship between father and child had been sacrificed on the altar of the secret love affair between her and Ike. Angela knew that she had offended her father and that the mental bruises the man sustained because of her misconduct, might never heal. Even if they healed, the vestiges would remain. That misbehaviour of hers had etched into her father's memory chambers never to erase.

"Nne, I'd rather have you talk to my father about this," Angela replied at last.

"Why?" Nnedi asked, her brow knitted.

Angela looked away dismally. Self-pity was written on her face. She never wanted to meet her father face to face with any problem concerning her personal life. Her father had written her off his good books, perhaps forever. Things were no longer the same. Although they were still biologically linked as father and child, but, symbiotically, they were miles apart. They hadn't been talking. Jacob, being a regimented and astute disciplinarian, would not allow time to heal the wounds his daughter inflicted on his ego.

"Why would you prefer me to tell your father your need? Is he no longer your father?" Nnedi asked, puzzled.

"He is my father legally," Angela replied hesitantly. She seemed to harbor some thoughts in her mind.

"What is that suppose to mean? Tell me, is anything wrong?" Nnedi asked in a most compassionate tone.

"Not really, but since that incident, papa doesn't relate well to me any more."

"What do you mean?"

Tears formed in her eyes. She fought it back. But her effort was fruitless.

"You slide into emotion so easily," Nnedi remarked. "I can't count the number of times you have shed tears in this one conversation."

She pulled Angela to her side affectionately and began to wipe her tears. "You must be a strong woman. You're too emotional my daughter. Stop crying, your eyes are turning red. Tell me, why can't you discuss your problem with your father?"

Angela wiped her eyes and said, "Since that *thing* happened, papa does not care about me any more. When I greet him, he doesn't acknowledge my greetings. When he does, it is so cold. When he sees me, he turns his face away. That bonding is no longer there. That attachment is no longer there. That petting and paternal affection he used to lavish on me, are all gone. Everything is done on a formal and distant level as if I were just one of the maids in the house. Even, the maids seem more important to him, can you believe that?

"He used to call me Nne, now he calls me Angela, and it sounds so incongruous in his mouth for my liking. Although he provides for me, that bonding and affection which I used to cherish, no longer exist. When he tries to be a little friendly, everything looks so mechanically contrived that even a child can discern that they were phony. In short, he hates me."

"I know what you mean my daughter," Nnedi said as she covered the little Ikechukwu with her head tie to ward off flies. "I can understand where you're coming from, but don't worry about all this. I know why he behaves the way he does, and I assume you know too..."

"But it's all over now," Angela whined. "Everything is over and should be done away with. Why does he have to torment me forever on that account?"

"I agree with you that everything is over, but the stain lives. That incident still resonates in his mind. *The rain has ceased, but the soil is still wet. The sore has healed, but the scar is there.* It will take a while for him to adjust and begin to relate to you the way he used to. I don't agree that he hates you. Maybe he dislikes what you did. I would say his reaction was natural. Anybody would react the same way. And this was chiefly because of the trust he reposed on you. He is still your father. The situation you have described will change with time. Time has mysterious ways of healing old wounds including the cracks in people's hearts. Your father will forget the incident. I know him, he is my son.

"Now stop worrying yourself about his not liking you. He is not your husband and he is not going to marry you, is he? He will begin to relate to you when he represses these ill feelings. And I guarantee you that before long he will forget everything. Now, as long as he provides your needs, don't worry about bonding and affection, they will come back at the right time. What about your mother?"

"I don't have much problem with mama, Angela replied. "Her case is manageable. At times she exhibits some ill feelings, but they are short-lived. For papa, ninety-nine percent of his behaviour towards me is driven by his feelings about my past mistake. When he wants to give me money, instead of giving it to me directly, he passes it through mama. Instead of giving me instructions directly, he channels them through mama. All this makes me feel like a stranger in my own home. This is why I want you to talk with him about my going to nursing school because he will not approve it if the idea is mine. He probably will like the nursing thing, and would want me to do it, but for the fact that the plan originated from me, he'd kick against it and would say, 'You are up again with your reckless ideas that often lands you in hell.' Everything I do these days is classified as abnormal and irresponsible. *If I operate from above, it's no good. If I operate from below, it's worse.* For example, if I'm sitting down, he'd say, 'why do you sit down always?' If I'm standing, he'd say, 'do you ever sit down?' There's nothing I do that will please papa. This attitude is indicative of his hatred on me."

Nnedi laughed.

"Nne, it's not funny." Angela said mournfully.

"Never mind my daughter. Leave that to me, I can handle it. I'll discuss it with him the next time he visits home. Just remind me before he leaves."

Nnedi pointed at the yellowish ball in the sky and cried, "Angie, look at the sun. The night is here. You and I have spent the whole day chatting."

"Nne, I like it so."

"I know you will like it, but shall we eat conversation?"

"I can forego meals listening to your genealogical narratives."

"I hear you. If we keep talking and chatting every day, how do we eat? Where would the food come from? Get up and go to the kitchen. But first, go to Izuagba's house…"

"To do what?" Angela snapped, raising her brows. She knew the man.

Nnedi staggered up from her chair with difficulty. She was in her mid eighties. She bent down and scooped Ikechukwu. She took the child to the door. She sat him on her feet, leaving a gap between the two feet. Ikechukwu began to urinate.

"Tell Izuagba to come here tomorrow morning to prune my palms," she instructed Angela.

"Is that all?" Angela said reluctantly, "Why don't I go there tomorrow morning?"

"No. Izuagba goes out very early," Nnedi explained. "You hardly meet him in the house in the morning."

"I see. Nne, make the fire for me so I can start cooking when I return."

"I will."

"But Nne, those palms are not ripe yet, are they?" Angela wondered

"They are ripe and had been falling off and wasting away." Nnedi said. "These days, it's difficult to get men to perform the men chores in the neighbourhood. It wasn't so in the past. This thing they call civilization is an ill-wind. God forbid! It is persistently blowing our young men away to the cities, leaving the village bereft of menfolk. If you have any men-jobs to do, you don't see anybody to help you. Years ago, you did not have to go to people's homes to seek for help. Young men stopped by every now and then. And they did these menial jobs free and out of goodwill. It's not so today. The avarice and attractions in the townships are gravitating young people to the cities and altering their philosophical disposition about life. Now go to Izuagba's place and tell him I want him to come here tomorrow and do some work for me."

Angela nodded her head but her face showed discontentment. Nnedi was always observant.

"Why do you frown?" she asked Angela.

"Nothing."

"But I can see your face. Don't you want to go?"

"I want to go. It's just that I hate that man."

"Angieee! Angieee!" Nnedi cried. "Why do you hate this one too? You hate Odunze, you hate Izuagba, who do you like? You seem to dislike everybody. *A crazy ship finds fault with every wind?* What's wrong with Izuagba a nice and benign man who helps every old woman in this village? What's wrong with him?'

"Nne, it's just that the man has a stupid way of looking at a person. It's disturbing. I dislike his character.

Nnedi stared at her grandchild for a moment. Isn't she too childish?" she thought, "very picky about men and their characters. Well, that's what girls do anyway. I believe that's how they size up men.

"Men naturally look at women," Nnedi explained, "especially beautiful women like you. He is probably admiring your good looks."

Angela smiled at that compliment. "I can distinguish admiration from a lustful gaze," she argued. "If he met you on the road, he would continue looking at you until you were out of sight. Worst of all, if you were talking to him, he'd focus his eyes on your chest area.

Nnedi burst into laughter. "Well, I don't know what to say in this case. You may be right, but all I know is that men have different reasons for looking at women. Either they are admiring your beauty or they are sizing you up for a potential future partner."

"For Izuagba, neither is the case," said Angela. "He's a salacious little man."

"I don't know about that. Whatever is the case, go to his house and tell him to come here tomorrow to dress up my palms. If he looks at you, ignore his eyes; deliver the message and leave. He cannot hold you spellbound with his eyes, I'm sure of that. Now go."

CHAPTER 11

On the day the Nzom guards caught Ike at the Okuiyi Ngene ponds, they hid him in the forest and waited for the dusk. They assumed Ike's people might be looking for him, and so they did not want to move him in the daylight. Their intention was to remove the captive at the cover of darkness and take him away.

At midnight, the guards crept out of the forest and headed for Umuiwu Nzom to deliver their captive to King Ekwealor Uyanne II of Umuiwu who needed human heads for the funeral of his late father, King Udedibia Uyanne I. King Ekwealor and his cabinet had deferred the burial ceremony of this great man because they needed three human heads to bury him. The cabinet believed that King Udedibia deserved a befitting burial which involved his interment with human heads.

To bury the dead with the living was a culture that was fast dying away in many parts of the world where it was practiced. The Nzom people and a few other towns in Nigeria also practiced the obnoxious tradition in those days. If King Ekwealor Uyanne were to bury his father without a human head, his people would laugh at him, and would call him a spineless King. In the eyes of the people, it would mean that his dead father had no responsible offspring to give him a befitting burial.

The dead King was a renowned traditional ruler. He had three titles of the land to his credit. His sons were determined to offer him a burial that was commensurate with his status in Nzom community. Each of the three titles required a male human head for his burial. The sacrificial victims must be slaughtered and their heads interred in the King's tomb.

The natives of Nzom were looking forward to the ceremony because it was an event of big feasting and merry-making. It was a once-in-a-life-time experience. Distant relatives and kinsmen were expected to attend. Many of them had not seen such a burial.

When the Nzom guards arrived at King Ekwealor Uyanne's palace at night, they presented the captive to him. He was so delighted that he paid the men double the fee. The guards were overjoyed because they had become rich overnight.

Ike was handed over to King Uyanne. Examining the captive, King Uyanne nodded his head approvingly and whispered to his men, "This is exactly what I want. He's young, hefty, and huge. The gods will accept the sacrifice without delay. Take him to the barn and make sure he is securely tied to the stable."

Ike did not know what fate awaited him. All transactions about him were privy to everybody except a few cabinet members. When the King's orderlies were trying to secure him to the stable, Ike was struggling and asking: "What have I done? What have I done?"

The barn where they kept Ike was nine hundred yards away from the King's castle. There were several barns within the vast compound, each of them built with tall thick mud-walls. King Uyanne's palace was huge and it contained many houses and small huts some of which belonged to his seven wives, children, and the servants.

In his cell, Ike was made to lie on his back. His hands and feet were fastened to four strong pillars. He did not know what he was there for. He thought his captors would release him after some punishment for stealing their fish. He was completely unaware of the King's secrete arrangements of human sacrifice.

Each barn was fenced all round with high mud walls, so that the prisoners could not scale over it. The narrow doorway was always in lock and guarded by security men.

All day and night Ike lay in this miserable state with the pains of his wound tormenting him. He waited patiently for his release. Little did he know that the only thing that stood between him and death was the availability of the third sacrificial man who was being hunted at moment. They had captured one earlier.

The King's daughter, Oliaku, fed the prisoners. King Uyanne had trained her daughter to perform some of the official duties like feeding special prisoners. The King trusted Oliaku so much that she handled most of his private matters.

At first, when they brought Ike into the prison, he refused to eat. Oliaku did not like this. Adrika, the first prisoner in the next barn, who was awaiting the same fate, ate very well. He even asked Oliaku for more. But Ike would not taste anything. He was consumed in misery over his present situation. All he wanted was his freedom.

Adrika was also fed in the mouth because his limbs were tied to the stake in the same position as Ike. He had been in captivity for several days before Ike arrived. In Adrika's case, he knew his fate. He ate as though he was in his house, gulping everything with relish. One day Oliaku asked him why he ate with unabated gusto knowing that he'd soon die. Adrika replied that since he knew he was going to die, he might as well enjoy his meal while he could. Oliaku was amused.

"If I refused to eat," he told Oliaku, "I'll die. If I eat, I'll die. Therefore, I prefer to eat and not suffer the pangs of hunger before I suffer the pangs of death. Oliaku saw some wisdom in the man's logic.

Adrika was in his late thirties, much older than Ike who was only twenty-two. He was a slim man. When they brought him to the prison, he cried all day and gradually resigned to his fate.

Back in his home town, Ntiji, Adrika had heard about the death of the famous King Udedibia Uyanne of Nzom. He also heard that his people were hunting for human heads with which to bury the King. So when he was captured while hunting in the forest near Nzom, he new he was gone.

In his cell, Ike lay pining away. His heart quaked with indignation. Three days had passed and he still refused to eat food. Each time the King's daughter, Oliaku, came in with his ration, he turned his face way. He never spoke to anyone. He never looked at people who came into his cell. His heart was filled with anger, hate, and confusion. Occasionally Oliaku tried to make him eat or at least talk, but Ike would not. He was in great distress. He wanted to be set free.

Ike remembered his mother and Emeka, his only brother with whom he went to Okuiyi Ngene to fish. Mentally, he recounted the incident that resulted in his capture. He wondered if Emeka made it home. He visualized Emeka standing at the precinct of the pond warning that it was unsafe to fish in Nzom ponds. He could hear Emeka arguing that he, Ike, had no knowledge of the rules guiding the Nzom fishing ponds.

Ike knew he caused his own misfortune. This was another big mistake in his life, and this one would be deadly, although he was yet to discover this. If he knew what would happen to him in the next few days, he would consider the incident at Onitsha a child's play. He still believed that his captors would release him, maybe after some torture and chastisement. But somehow, after recalling what Emeka had told him about some trespassers being killed at the private ponds in Nzom, he began to fear.

Emeka warned me, Ike reprimanded himself as he lay brooding over his plight. If I had listened to him; if I had taken his advice; if we had gone to Ochula pond to fish; this would not have happened. Where would Emeka be now? Did they capture him too, or did he escape? Where is my brother? Oooooh! Emeka, Emeka, Emekaooooo!

Tears.

CHAPTER 12

The following day Oliaku brought food to feed Ike. As usual, he refused to eat. The girl became upset.

"Why won't you eat?" she shouted at Ike angrily. "Do you want to die before the time?"

Ike held his breath. A strange tingle ran through his spine. "Die before the time?" he repeated in his heart. This struck him hard. He was startled. He turned his head for the first time looking at Oliaku's direction. What does she mean by 'die before the time?' Before what time? Before the time, before the time; he kept repeating in his heart.

He tried to raise his head, but he couldn't. There was a sharp pain on his shoulder. He turned again and looked at Oliaku. That was the first time Ike had looked at the girl in the face. Does this mean I'm actually going to die here? he thought. Does it mean I'm waiting to be killed? So I'm going to die in the hands of these brutes?

His heart began to pound harder, quivering with the pangs of remorse. He wished that the incident at Okuiyi had not taken place. He wished that things could be reversed. There was no way he could contact his people for help. He had no communication with anybody except the King's daughter who came to his cell to feed him.

Oliaku noticed the shock on Ike's face following her comment. She realized that the statement she made about "dying before the time" had evoked anxiety in this man. She perceived a feeling of fear, suspicion, and confusion in him. She realized that the prisoner did not even know why he was being detained.

"What did you say?" Ike asked the girl between trembling lips. That was the first time he spoke.

When Ike spoke, Oliaku knew the ethnic group he belonged to. His accent was that of Okpanam, the natives where her grandmother came from. Ike's dialect was the same as her grandmother's.

Oliaku began to view the prisoner with a mixture of anger and curiosity.

"Oh, you can now speak?" she said rudely. "I've been talking to you for the past three days, but you didn't want to respond. Do you feel you can talk now? What made you decide to talk? You might as well eat."

Ike did not reply, instead he looked away. His anger and hatred went up. His heartbeat rose with astounding rapidity. His brain whirled round and round in turmoil. As he summarized Oliaku's statements inwardly, his emotion kept oscillating between indignation and despondency. He wished he could free himself. But the bands that held him onto the pillars were too strong to be broken by sheer human strength. Not even the stamina of a superman could break the ropes. His limbs were beginning to swell and the rope was eating into his skin, almost shutting off circulation.

"Since they brought you here," Oliaku began, "you have not eaten anything; you don't want to eat; you don't want to talk; you keep ignoring everybody. The prisoner in the other barn eats very well. He talks too, even though he is aware of what will happen to him. Do you understand why you are here? You had better take some food. In any case, whether you eat or not..."

Oliaku cut short her words when Ike switched his head to her direction to hear the rest of her comments.

Real fear gripped Ike. "What will happen?" he asked the girl.

"They will kill you. Your life is hanging by a thread."

Ike's heart stopped. He became restless and began to sweat. When his heart finally resumed beating, the speed was alarming.

"Kill me for what?" he asked the girl. "Which people will kill me?"

"Does it matter?" she replied sarcastically. "You'll die whether you eat food or not."

When Ike realized why he was cast into prison, his spirit crumbled. His heart sank into the depths of his guts. His trunk shook convulsively. This frightened Oliaku.

She picked up her food and hurried off thinking that the prisoner was dying following her disclosure. She regretted giving out the secret.

Well, he may eat if he wanted, Oliaku said to herself after leaving the barn, it doesn't really matter. *Is there any sense in renovating a house that will soon be demolished?*

The prison where Ike was kept had no roof, but there were small trees in the barn that offered cover against the elements. The foliage of the trees was so dense that there was hardly any opening to let in daylight. He stared above. The branches swayed at intervals revealing small openings. Long arrows of the sun pierced through these openings stabbing him like the sharp spear of the guards at Okuiyi. But these stabs were harmless.

CHAPTER 13

Now, Ike was almost certain he was going to die. This fact was inadvertently revealed to him by the girl who fed the prisoners. He had come to grips with the idea behind his captivity. He feared that his captors would soon murder him. For what reason? he kept wondering.

He looked up above. He couldn't control the flow of tears - tears of anguish. He sobbed and pulsated. Suddenly the door of the barn flung open. The gateman ushered in a team of royalties led by King Uyanne himself. Ike immediately concluded that his time was up. They have come to kill me, he said to himself. His heart-beat accelerated and he quivered.

Once in a while, King Uyanne went to the cells for a routine inspection. Today two title holders accompanied him. They stood around the prisoner and studied him.

Ike watched them carefully in terror. He observed that the monarchs were all huge men with towering personalities. All of them had their chieftaincy horse-tails in their hands. Ike had no difficulty identifying the

King amongst the retinue, for King Uyanne's chieftaincy regalia distinguished him from the rest of the entourage.

The King had earlier been informed that this prisoner was not eating. He and his cabinet members examined Ike closely. Ike's stomach was flabby but he looked healthy and vivacious.

The King looked at his men and made a sign. They moved out of Ike's ear-shot.

"Quite suitable for the purpose, isn't he?" The King said.

"Precisely!" agreed the men, "he's quite good for the purpose."

"I received a report that he does not eat," said the King, "do you think he will survive till the date?"

"Definitely," said one of the chiefs, "he will be alive, even if he does not eat at all. But they should try to make him eat."

"He's a young man full of vitality," the other crowned head observed. "He won't die.

When they got to the gate, the gateman said to the King, "Your Highness, this one has refused to eat since they brought him."

"Tell them to find a way to make him eat."

"All right, your Highness."

Ike did not need a soothsayer to decipher what was going on and what would soon happen to him. Although he didn't hear a word of their whispering, his intuition told him what was amiss. He knew his days were numbered. He knew *there was a snake in the fiber.* His heart kept beating fast as his faith wavered. He thought that his chances of surviving this ordeal were zero. His tears flowed more often than ever. He became apprehensive and freaked at every movement.

Again, Oliaku came with Ike's food. She met him crying. Tears were pouring down his cheeks. It was a pathetic sight for the young maiden. Her heart sank empathically. She cast a piteous look at the prisoner staring at him the way she had never done before. She was speechless for a while, and then she said:

"What are you doing?"

Ike did not answer. Instead, he resented the girl's presence. He did not want to be seen crying, definitely not by a young woman. Oliaku's questions aggravated and intensified his emotion.

The girl sat down on a stone at the corner and watched him. Several emotion-provoking thoughts ran across her mind as she gazed balefully at Ike pouring out painful tears. She seldom saw a man cry. Ike's tears were coming down like rain. She knew that those were tears of fear and hopelessness.

He never cried like this before, Oliaku thought as she watched him. He is cute, tall, hefty, and energetic. He hasn't eaten for days, yet he looks so fresh and robust. He is so young to be sacrificed to the gods. They should've got an older man.

"What are you doing?" she asked Ike again.

It's pathetic to see men cry. Men are expected to handle emotions. Women shed tears easily. An old woman once said: "women have their tear-pouch sitting right above their eye-lids. The slightest provocation can open the floodgate. But men can endure."

Men can hold tears. It was heart-melting for Oliaku to watch Ike shed tears in this agonizing way. The sight was taking a toll on the eighteen year old daughter of the King. Pathetic tears loomed in her own eyes. Quickly, she collected the uneaten food and left. As she was going, she wiped her eyes clean, lest they might ask her why she was crying, and she'd not be able to explain.

That night, Ike reviewed all that had happened recently. He recapped what Oliaku said: '...do you want to die before the time? In any case, whether you eat or not...' He thought about the visit of the King and his men. Summing up these things, he believed they were planning something callous. The way they looked at me portends ominous sign, he told himself.

That night, as he lay in his dungeon thinking about his death, he suddenly felt quickened by some ethereal power. His fears vanished.

He became more irritated than fearful. His hatred against the people who kept him in bondage heightened. Strong mental frame began to emerge, and instead of dwelling on thoughts about what will happen to him, he decided to think about survival. He began to talk to himself:

Now that you know you're going to die, what do you do? How can you escape? Who will help you do so? Who will cut these ropes? Can you see your people again or would you end up dying here? How can you connect your people to rescue you? Oh! Emeka is not close. I wish he could hear me. I wish he could organize our men to save me. Oooooh!

It was an uphill task for Ike to put aside the crippling thoughts about his death and to concentrate on survival strategies. His brain was in turmoil. He was unable to articulate his thoughts about a get-away plan.

He wrestled with this situation for a long time and finally decided to embark on an escape plan. If I succeeded, he told himself, thank God; if not, so be it. I can only die but once. Besides, *'death is a necessary end that must come when it will come.'* I read this in Julius Caesar. I prefer to die fighting for my life. Only trees stand still when they are threatened; most creatures run to save their lives, how much more humans?

With these thoughts, Ike felt strong again. A sense of relief descended on him. His tension eased, and his nerves that had stood on edge, relaxed. He even slept for the first time since his captivity.

Ike's sleep was interrupted in the morning when Oliaku came with his breakfast. Surprisingly, he allowed the girl to feed him. He ate up everything and even requested for more. That was the first time he tasted food since he was captured. He had been starving himself in a quiet protestation, hoping that this course of action would attract sympathy from his captors. Oliaku had been bitter about his refusal to eat. Today she was happy.

Delighted about this, Oliaku went for more food. There was no food left in the kitchen. Everything was gone, but because she was excited, she volunteered her food.

At the entrance of the barn, the guard saw Oliaku with the second plate and said, "Why?"

Oliaku ignored the gateman. The food was obviously different from what prisoners were served, and the guard saw it.

"Where are you going with that food?" the man insisted as Oliaku crossed his post.

"Is it part of your duty to check the dispensation of food?" Oliaku snapped. "Mind your business."

She passed the gateman and went in to feed Ike. Ike devoured everything and felt much better. Except for the pains from his shoulder wound, he felt strong and energized.

He began to beam with a new spirit as if he had been granted freedom. Oliaku noticed the change and was happy. But her joy was tinged with despair and deep-rooted empathy because she knew what would soon happen. She began to think:

Very soon this robust young man will be slaughtered and his head buried with the dead King - an old man who lived ninety-eight years. Stupid! Obnoxious culture! I hate this thing.

She was deeply worried. She had suddenly developed an antithetic opinion about this aspect of her people's culture. As she surveyed the imposing carriage lying in front of her, she asked herself:

What is the meaning of this sacrifice? If a dead man is buried with the head of a living man, of what value is it? What does the dead King gain, and what does the living gain? Would the sacrifice prevent the dead man's offspring from dying?

She ran her eyes over Ike's huge trunk. His entire physical appearance was strong, but as tender as the yam tendril, and as fresh as the cocoa-yam leaves at the peak of the rainy season. She looked at Ike's long limbs strewn with veins. His legs were stout and muscularly. He was about six feet eleven. He was radiating energy. What a carriage! Oliaku thought.

How can this man die without committing any crime? Why? Why must he die?

But an internal voice rebuked her saying: "What do you know about the custom of Nzom? This is an honour bestowed to eminent Kings like your grandfather. Your ancestors approved it, why can't your father do it for his late father? And besides, this is men's affair. It is not women business. Shut up and leave."

Oliaku obeyed the voice in her heart. She packed her plates and went in.

CHAPTER 14

In the evening, Oliaku showed up with Ike's supper. Again he ate up everything. Oliaku was happy. She watched him sympathetically as a mother would watch a sick child. She said,

"Is it okay if I ask how you feel today?"

Ike ignored her and swung his face the other way.

"Won't you talk to me?" Oliaku said tenderly. "You talked to me the other day."

She felt sad about Ike's suffering. She was compassionate. She wanted to open up conversation with this man to know who he was, but Ike was not interested. He was preoccupied with the thoughts about his safety. He had been told about his fate in a clear language.

"What's your name?" Oliaku insisted.

Ike looked at her briefly and turned away with a frown. His heart ached with a burden of unshed tears. He hadn't cried today.

"Pardon me to say that this is not a constructive attitude," Oliaku attacked.

Ike mumbled something.

"What did you say?" the girl asked anxiously.

There was no reply.

"What did you say just now?"

"Nothing." Ike snarled.

Oliaku's face glittered with joy. "I'm glad you spoke to me. I was saying you should try to adopt a better attitude. My name is Oliaku. What is your name?"

Silence.

Oliaku was eager to have him say something, no matter what.

"Would you present a better behaviour and a kinder attitude?"

Silence.

"I presume you don't have good etiquette."

"Which attitude is more appropriate in this circumstance? You brute!" Ike snapped and turned his face away.

Oliaku was quiet for a few minutes, and then she went over to the other side to see his face. But Ike turned back his face. She came over again where his face was. Ike turned away again.

Oliaku felt beaten on the drama and said,

"Do you think it's my fault that you're here in tether? I'm only trying to be friendly."

"You are an enemy. You're one of them."

"I am not, I'm only a woman."

"Women are part of the system of crude and cruel culture. Go away! I hate you and your people."

"But women have no say, neither in the making nor in the implementation of the laws of the land. It is the men."

Silence.

Oliaku seemed to recognize some truth in Ike's indictment. Both men and women are integral parts of a system. Nevertheless, she still believed that the import and implication of their custom were none of her business. She kept quiet allowing a little time to elapse. And then she said,

"Your heart is loaded with anger and hate. Don't think that I'm insensitive to your situation. Don't you think it would be appropriate to see things differently?"

"That is when you have an option. I have no option."

"I asked you to tell me your name," Oliaku said. Her voice was soft and benign. She tried to be as friendly as possible. Although she was a young girl, she was able to muster the strategies that women apply to force men to act. "Tell me your name young man."

"What for?" Ike retorted loudly. "What has my name got to do with my death? Why don't you pack your dishes and leave?"

His face bared the anger and distress in his heart. Oliaku saw it.

"Not until you have told me your name," said the girl defiantly.

"Nuisance!" Ike cursed.

"Handsome, what's your name?" Oliaku insisted whimsically.

Ike felt irritated with this confrontation. He knew it wasn't part of her duty to interrogate him. The pain from his wound was also exasperating.

It was also Oliaku's assignment to dress Ike's wound. Every morning she went to the shrub, plucked some leaves, squeezed them, and dropped the sap on the wound. She also pasted the mashed pulp of the leaves on the face of the wound.

The herbs had excellent healing property. Within a few days after his arrival, the wound had begun to heal. But it was still painful. Ike was lucky the spear didn't touch his shoulder blade.

"Talk to me," Oliaku persisted. "I'm only trying to be friendly. I've been nice to you, haven't I? I feed you daily. I dress your wound and I give you special attention more than I give other prisoners. Do you know that? Be a little sensible."

Truly, Oliaku was giving Ike special attention. She wanted Ike to understand this and reciprocate. Ike thought for a moment trying to sift some truth in what the girl was saying. But he was still bitter. The fair treatment had nothing to do with his primary concern – freedom.

"Whether I tell you my name or not, what difference does it make in my fate? I am going to die. You brutes want to kill me, what is the need listening to your useless prattles? I want to be left alone. You may leave?"

"I know your circumstance," Oliaku said solemnly, "but at least you're alive today. You're breathing now."

"So?"

Oliaku had nothing to say in reply to that monosyllabic question.

"Has my name anything to do with my safety?"

"Just curiosity. Tell me," she pleaded.

"Nonsense!"

"Tell me, please," Oliaku coaxed almost babyishly.

"I guess you're old enough to know what awaits me," Ike said, showing irritability. "You should understand that my life is at stake. This is not a good time for jokes. My days are numbered and you know it. Leave this place and go to your barbaric hoodlums who are planning to kill me?"

Oliaku had no answer. She knew Ike was right.

Another silence.

Oliaku was hesitant to press on. She told Ike that his wound was healing very well. Maybe that would soften his heart. Ike ignored her. Whether his wound healed or not, he was going to die with it. What's the difference? *Is there any rationale in mending a house slated for destruction, who cares?* he thought.

A long pause was followed by the same question from Oliaku, "What's your name?" to which Ike surprisingly responded,

"My name is Ikechukwu."

Oliaku smiled revealing a set of snow-white teeth. She was a beautiful girl with a charming face. She was ebony black and tall. On both sides of her cheeks sat two glorious dimples that could hold water. At eighteen, she was in her full bloom.

She bent over and flipped off a fly that was buzzing on Ike's wound.

"Ikechukwu," she repeated softly, her face beaming with smile. Her persistence had paid off. "That's a nice name. Ikechukwu where are you from?"

"Again?" Ike snapped. "I expect you should go after I told you my name. Is disturbing me part of your assignments?"

"Ikechukwu, be a little sensible," Oliaku fought back, cautiously though. She didn't want to damage the relationship that was developing.

Ike tried to adjust his position but his shoulder was hurting. He grimaced and heaved a sigh of anguish. Oliaku observed this and said,

"Sorry."

Ike didn't acknowledge.

She kept looking at Ike as he reeled in pain. She wanted to ask him about the pain, but she was afraid he'd complain of disturbance. Ike had told her his name and she considered it enough for now.

The girl seemed to enjoy the little rapport building between her and the prisoner. She knew that if the relationship was to grow, she must nurture it. She was tempted to talk to him again,

"I understand your situation, but try to be a little friendly. I'm only trying to make you feel better. Why are you so blunt and hostile to me?"

"I know you are a child, but..."

"No no no! don't ever call me a child," Oliaku interrupted, pointing a finger at Ike. "Who is a child?"

"I was going to say you were mature enough to realize the critical situation I was in," Ike veered a little. "You should understand that someone in a grave condition have no room for puerility. Need I to look at things from any perspective other than the perspective of my death? For once, imagine yourself in my situation. I would rather die thinking about my fate than answering your useless questions. I have told you my name, can I have a breathing space?"

"Ikechukwu, what appears as a disturbance is just the little way I can demonstrate my concern for your plight. I don't mean to add more to your distress."

"If my situation wasn't a matter of life and death, you might be right and I can afford to entertain your frivolities. But this is a grave situation. *You don't sleep with particles in your eyes, do you?*"

"Meaning?"

"*A person whose house is on fire does not chase rats.* I've to think about my death."

He was right, Oliaku admitted inwardly. He uses idioms and metaphors. He must be intelligent.

She studied Ike for a while.

Ike looked up. He couldn't see the sky. The trees shielded the sky and the world away from him. Yes, she is the only friend I have in the world right now, Ike thought. But of what use is she?

At this point, a voice spoke to Ike in his heart: "Don't be pessimistic, think positively. This girl is not an enemy. If anything could be done to save your life, it can hardly come from any source other than this young woman. You don't understand, but she is the closest person to you today. If you have any hope of coming out of this ordeal alive, she could be an instrument."

Ike began to turn this statement over in his heart. He was a smart and articulate individual, but the gravity of his ordeal did not allow his cognitive processes to run the right and straight course. He repeated what the inner voice had just whispered to him, 'This girl is the only person you can count on.'

He summoned courage and asked Oliaku,

"Do you remember I asked you yesterday who were going to kill me and how I was going to be killed?"

"Yes, I remember," Oliaku answered readily and lurched forward to hear more. She was always enthusiastic whenever Ike spoke.

"But you declined to discuss that," Ike continued. "That's what will interest me. You told me it didn't make any difference who was going to kill me or how I was going to die. You said the bottom-line was that, come what may, I was going to die. Is that not true? Can you tell me everything you know about my fate?"

"Let me go to the bush and pluck some leaves for your wound," Oliaku said obediently with a sense of duty. "I will explain everything when I come back."

CHAPTER 15

Meanwhile, the preparation for King Udedibia Uyanne's funeral was in full swing. Dance groups and drummers in the thirteen villages of Nzom were rehearsing their songs. But King Uyanne was still stuck with finding one more person for the human sacrifice. He had got two men, Adrika and Ike. His agents were desperately hunting for the third head. He must bury his father with three human heads. He would pay any price for this.

When Oliaku had gone to pluck the herbs, Ike began to talk to himself:

Your salvation lies in this girl. If there's anybody that could be instrumental to your escape, she's the one. If there's anything that could be done to save your life, she has the key. She's in sympathy with you, this is a good sign. If you try, you might win her confidence, and both of you could work out something. There is no other way.

Following this self-counseling exercise, Ike began to think seriously about re-gaining his freedom. As he was marshalling out these instructions to himself, Oliaku returned from the bush. She folded her waist wrapper half way up her thigh revealing her pretty legs. It was a graceful sight. Ike saw her awesome thighs, but he was not in the mood. This was the last thing he wanted to think about at this critical moment. *One whose house is on fire does not chase rats.* Nevertheless, he took one quick look at the succulent legs and sighed.

Oliaku mashed the fresh leaves in her palms and dressed Ike's wound. She observed that the wound was fast healing. It was only the size of a six-penny coin now. The treatment was effective and Ike's system was resilient too. In a short time the wound would be gone and the crushing pain with it. Most children knew medicinal leaves, especially children whose parents and grandparent practiced traditional medicine. The art was passed from generation to generation.

After the treatment, Oliaku sat on the stone beside Ike. She comported herself in an exquisite feminine manner. Lately, she had been treating Ike like a friend rather than an enemy.

"My grandfather died two months ago," she began. "It's a strong custom of the Nzom people that when a prominent king dies, he must be buried with human heads. This way, his ancestors would welcome him into their ancestral fold in the land of the dead. This is a rite that cannot be done without, neither can it be compromised. It must be performed. If not, the spirit of the dead King will continue to haunt his children who are supposed to carry out the ritual. Also, the man's children are regarded as spineless folks who cannot give their father a befitting burial.

"If my father fails to fulfill this obligation, not only that he would not be recognized by his people, but he stands the danger of loosing his throne. For this reason, he had commissioned agents to kidnap men whose heads must be used to perform the burial ceremony.

"My father is an influential King. Even when his father, King Udedibia Uyanne, was alive, he was already powerful and famous. He is a tough man whose influence has no boundary. Before his father died, he promised him he was going to perform the ritual for him. Therefore, to forego it, is out of the question. The King is poised to accomplish it, come rain, come sunshine.

"Regarding your case, my father caught the wind that some strangers were being captured at Okuiyi Ngene fishing ponds. There's nothing my father wanted in this town that he could not get. He bargained with the guards of the ponds promising them reward if they could bring him someone. And they succeeded in getting one for him. Ike, you're the one. Were you not captured at Okuiyi Ngene?"

Ike looked at Oliaku and sighed. He knew her story was authentic.

"That's precisely why you're lying here today. The guards at the pond sold you to my father for the burial sacrifice."

Oliaku paused and studied Ike's reaction. Nothing out of the ordinary seemed to happen. Ike was loaded with hatred and fear. But he was pleased that the girl revealed these things to him. Some of the King's inner cabinet members did not know about this story.

"The guards who sold you to my father," Oliaku continued, "said there were two fishermen in the pond. They got you, but the other man escaped. Is that not true?"

Ike did not speak. He knew that the other man was his brother, Emeka. He remembered Emeka at that point and wondered what might have happened to him. Did he escape and ran home? he thought. Is he alive or dead? He wished he knew Emeka's fate. For a moment, he forgot about himself, and thought about Emeka and what might have happened to him.

"Three heads are needed for the ritual," Oliaku went on, "two heads have been secured. They need one more person, after which the human sacrifice will be performed."

Her story, though factual, did not provoke visible fear in Ike. Instead, she noticed a short grin that portrayed the bitterness in his heart. She knew that beneath this grin, was a smoldering laver.

"Does my story sound funny?" she asked Ike.

"No," he replied.

"Then why are you smiling?"

"Because I don't think I'll die," he said stoutly.

Oliaku stared at him puzzled.

What does he mean? she thought. Did I hear him correctly?

"What did you say?"

"I'll not die." Ike repeated, tears threatening. He fought the tears back. He warned himself that tears would not be of any help at this point.

Oliaku had noticed the tears in his eyes looming like rain in the cloud. But it did not rain. Ike subdued it. She too was close to dropping a tear. Tears are sometimes contagious.

Oliaku surveyed Ike carefully as he lay on the ground helpless, hands and legs fastened to four hefty pillars. She summed up his imposing carriage and wondered why he said he would not die. Is he a strong man? she thought. He must be delusional.

"What makes you think that you'll not die?" She broke the silence, still puzzled. "Don't you believe my story?"

"I don't doubt a word of your story," Ike replied, "but I cannot die here. They won't kill me. Never!"

Is it bravery or stupidity? Oliaku thought. I must go, he is mad.

She got up to leave but changed her mind. She looked at Ike reflectively. She seemed to admire his valour but concluded that courage was of no use to him now. "You are foolish!" she said.

"Maybe, but I'll get back home," Ike affirmed. His voice was strong.

"You seem to have a dangerous ego that borders on insanity. What do you mean 'I will not die?' You might think I was joking. I thought that after listening to my story you would be terrified. Listen to me, you're facing death, you will soon die! Why should you allow your ego to get into this? Are you sure you understand our dialect?"

"I do," Ike replied solemnly, his voice resolute. "I understand all you said, but I'm telling you that I have the conviction that I'll not die here. I'll not die in the hands of your father and his co-murderers. I have done nothing wrong. I'll see my people again."

Oliaku became more confused at Ike's outburst. How can he do it? she thought. How can he loose these bands to set himself free? Perhaps his people practice witchcraft. Perhaps his father is a medicine man and may use some remote charms to rescue him. If that is the case, he had better hurry up and alert his people.

"Do you mean you'll see your people in spirit when you die?" Oliaku asked.

"In flesh," replied Ike.

"How?"

"I will."

"I said how!" she shouted, almost upset.

"I don't know, but I will."

Oliaku became a little angry at his senseless display of bravery. She managed a cynical smile laced with irritation. In her heart, she believed Ike was not only stubborn but also witless. How on earth can someone in the lion's mouth make merry? she thought.

"I have never seen such a fool," she told Ike. "Are you sure you are in your senses?"

"I am mentally fit," Ike replied, "and I mean what I said. I'll be home."

"You are tied here with a strong band. There's no way you can loose this rope to gain your freedom. Besides, your hands and feet are swollen. How can you escape?"

There was another silence, a protracted one. Then Ike said nervously, "Do you want me to die?"

Oliaku stared at him for a moment with a mixture of passion and confusion. She observed the solicitous note in

Ike's voice. She didn't know what answer to give to that simple question.

Oliaku had developed a little attachment on this prisoner. She had been entertaining pitiful emotions. But she never allowed these feelings to manifest in her behaviour. She must not let emotions interfere with her duty. Nobody must know it, not even Ike, or else she'd be in danger. Her father was a heartless monarch, a ruthless autocrat, and a brute tyrant. He had killed many people for a simple mistake. Her sympathy or emotions for the young man must be hidden deep in her heart.

"Your death has nothing to do with me," she finally said, evasively. "I'm only here to feed you and to dress your wound. Why should you ask me whether I want you to die?"

"That doesn't answer my question," Ike said. "My question is: Do you want me to die? As a human being with a conscience, would you personally like to see me die under this obnoxious circumstance?"

"It's the custom and tradition of our people. I have nothing to do with the burial ritual. It's none of my business. Remember, I'm a woman."

Ike observed that Oliaku was still evading the question. She was unwilling to bring herself to the core of the matter. Ike wanted her to say: 'Really I don't want you to die. I hate to see it happen, but...' He would then cash in and solicit her cooperation in planning his escape. But Oliaku was smart. She avoided proffering an answer that was capable of roping her in. She did not want to commit herself to anything.

Ike did not want to press any further for fear of losing her assistance completely.

"I know you are a woman," Ike said cautiously, "but women can do heroic things. Women have powers and they can achieve great fits. Listen, what's your name?"

"Oliaku." The girl replied.

"Oliaku, I have something to discuss with you. First, do me a favour."

Her heart jumped. She thought Ike was going to ask her to set him free.

"What?" she replied quickly.

"Can you keep a secret?"

"Can I keep a secret? What secret?"

"I want you to keep this conversation between you and me secret. Don't say anything to anybody. That's the favour I'm requesting of you."

"Is that all?"

"That's all for now."

"That's simple. Even if you didn't tell me, I won't tell anybody."

"Are you sure?"

"I won't talk," Oliaku assured him.

"My life hangs on this pledge," Ike stressed.

"I promise, I won't talk."

"I trust you. I believe you won't tell anybody. I'll rest my fate upon your promise. I see you as a bold and courageous woman who has understanding and human sympathy; a woman who could brave dangers; a woman that can stand for the truth; a woman that would not allow innocent blood to be shed; a woman whose love can cut cords; and a woman whose affection transcends cultural and traditional barriers.

"I appreciate the fair treatment you have shown to me all along. Most importantly, I thank you for your love and care. "I also admire your beauty. Pardon me to say that it's only now that I realized how pretty you are. I have never seen such a charming image in my life. But let's put this aside for the moment.

"Now, collect your plates and go. You have overstayed. Your people might suspect you're talking to me. When you come back tomorrow, I'll unveil my plans to you. Remember, don't disclose this matter. Keep it to yourself."

Obediently the girl picked up her plates and left.

At the gate the guard saw her and said, "Are you still there? What have you been doing?"

Oliaku scowled at the gateman. "Look here Anyadike, I have warned you to mind your business. So far, the King has not informed me that your assignment includes monitoring my movements or checking how much time I spend feeding the prisoners and dressing their wounds? If you want to keep your job, be careful or else you'll know *what the flame can do to the rat's ears.*"

The gateman was shaken. He pleaded with Oliaku to forget the matter, promising he'd never talk to her again on this issue. He knew that if she launched a complaint against him, the King would dismiss him without asking questions. King Uyanne invested a lot of confidence on his daughter. Oliaku commanded an unusual influence in the sight of the King.

CHAPTER 16

The large trunk of the Opel Record was full so that the lid could not close. Then Ufele instructed his boys to pack the rest of the luggage in the back seat of his car. He was going to the village to get first-hand information about what happened to Ike. He heard that Ike was kidnapped or killed by the Nzom people at Okuiyi Ngene ponds. The news was a bombshell to his family. Everybody was sad and distressed except Alfred, his son.

Alfred had moved to his own house about a year ago after he started work. Occasionally he stopped by to see his parents, especially when he needed something from them. His father was rich. This evening, he was visiting when the sad news came that Ike was missing. Ufele and his family were thrown into grief. Akuoma, Ufele's wife, cried bitterly. She told her husband she had heard that some kidnapers were hunting human heads to bury a dead King at one of the river-rine towns.

Alfred was indifferent to their empathic reactions to the sad news. He laughed and raised his fist, "That serves him right," he retorted.

His parents were astonished at that remark. Alfred was still nursing the ill-feelings he had against Ike when they were teenagers. He hadn't forgotten anything even at his mature age now. He hated Ike, in fact, he wanted him to die.

"What's funny about this sad news Alfred?" said his mother puzzled. "What's funny about the report that your cousin was missing? Is it a laughing matter?"

"Let him die." Alfred said, and picked up his cap and left.

Akuoma wasn't surprised. She knew that Alfred did not like Ike right from the beginning. She knew that the childhood bitterness Alfred held against his cousin was still in his system like a cancerous tumor. He hated Ike and would like him to perish in the hands of his captors.

The apprentice boys were equally hit by the sad news. They gathered in their room and discussed the matter. They felt so bad about the misfortune of their former colleague. On the very day they heard the news, there was no cracking of jokes, no laughing, no music, no enjoyment, and no discussions. Most of the boys did not eat. Some of them were crying. The entire Ufele household was thrown into mourning. The atmosphere was tepid and apathetic. Faces were latticed with grief. Every conversation was about Ike's calamity.

CHAPTER 17

On the fourth day of his captivity, Ike had begun to plan his escape. His survival instincts had come into play in earnest. The previous night he was constructing and restructuring the strategies for his escape. He didn't sleep. In order to free himself, he must obtain the collaboration of the young maiden who fed him. Her full participation was sine qua non for his freedom, and he was working on this.

The important questions revolving in his mind were: Would Oliaku consent to work with him, seeing she was part of the arrangement to sacrifice him to the gods? Suppose she became frightened about the plot and gave away the secret to her people? How would he make certain that she would not be *running with the hare and chasing with the hound?* These were the bugging questions in Ike's mind as he lay awake thinking about his survival.

Judging from the degree of relationship that had developed between him and the girl, and her compassionate disposition towards him lately, Ike felt that he could count on Oliaku's support. He believed she would not give up the secret and would do whatever he asked her to do. Nevertheless, he cautioned himself to be meticulous and tactful, not taking anything for granted.

He knew that he must be truly friendly with this young woman, as opposed to being hostile and aggressive - the position he had been espousing since his capture. He must also control his anger and animosity against his captors. Of equal importance was the need to pay close attention to the movements of people. He should watch everybody, even Oliaku herself. He did not know her well yet.

Soon afterwards Oliaku arrived with Ike's breakfast. As she entered the gate, she beamed a smile to Ike who interpreted the smile to mean that everything was falling into shape. This is a good sign, Ike thought. To Oliaku, however, the significance of her smile was an expectation that Ike would eat her food, nothing more. Ike tried to smile back but his smile was too artificial to warm a heart. All the same, Oliaku treasured it. After all, she had never seen a smile on his face. She understood. *A man whose house is on fire does not chase rats.*

When Ike had eaten, Oliaku sat down on the stone and listened to him. Following their last conversation, she knew he had something to tell her. Since she developed a special interest in Ike's situation, she fed other prisoners first before attending to Ike because she knew she'd spend more time with him. She was beginning to enjoy his company. However, she did these things very carefully mindful that some people might be watching. She didn't want to create the impression that she had a soft spot for his father's prisoner. As she took her seat, she wondered what Ike was going to say. Ike began,

"First, I must thank you for being a very caring and sympathetic individual," he spoke in a very low tone. "I cannot adequately express my appreciation to you for the kindness and understanding you have shown so far towards my circumstance. I appreciate all your concerns and hope that you'll sustain it till the end. Secondly, I want to remind you about my determination to regain my freedom. You'll remember that I told you I don't want to die here. I believe that I'll get back to my people. This might sound pretentious to you, but that's what I have resolved to do. I'm determined to secure my freedom come rain, come sunshine, and I would rather die doing so than stay here and allow your people to slaughter me like a ram."

Oliaku wondered how he was going to do that. She ran her eyes over Ike's figure, focusing on the bands that held the man to the posts. Talking to herself, Oliaku said: how is he going to loose these bands to regain his freedom; how does he intend to free himself? What magic does he possess?

"When I told you I must get back to my village," Ike went on, "you asked me how I was going to do it. I told you then that I was going to disclose my plans to you today. Now listen carefully, you're going to help me..."

"What!" Oliaku shouted convulsively and rose to her feet. "Me, to do what?"

Her face changed immediately. This reaction truly betrayed her as an enemy and an integral part of the obnoxious culture. This was clearly written on her face. She wanted to run, but Ike calmed her down.

"Be patient. You're the only human being that can save my life," Ike said firmly. He didn't mince words.

Oliaku stared at him terrified. She kept looking at Ike incredulously as though he was having a psychotic episode. "How can...? No!"

"Don't rush, I'll explain. Sit down. I look at you as someone who is articulate and understanding; one who has the courage to stand up against evil; and one who can condemn injustice. I'm here today face-to-face with death because I fished in the ponds that belonged to the Nzom natives. I made a mistake, I admit. I was away to the city for a long period of time. I forgot all about the rules and regulations guiding the fishing business among the neighbouring towns. Thus, I went fishing in the Nzom pond and was caught.

"When I was younger, we fished in the neighbours' ponds. We trespassed the neighbours' properties, rampaged their farms and got away with it. All they did was chase us away like crop-menacing birds or whip us if they caught us. There was no killing, nor serious injury. But today, the story is different. Until you revealed my fate, I didn't know I was going to be killed. I thought they would only punish and release me. I didn't know that the Nzom fishermen who captured me sold me for a ritual sacrifice to the gods. Right now, my people do not know where I am or what is about to happen to me. But I'm not scared because I know I'll not die. I must go home."

Oliaku stared at him puzzled. Any time Ike said he wasn't going to die, the girl looked at him in amazement as if he was hallucinating. She wondered how he was going to free himself.

"Your courage amazes me," she said contumeliously. "However, How... What do you mean by you're not going to die? How are you going to save yourself?"

"That's what we're here to discuss. You're going to assist me."

"Me!" Oliaku exploded again, pointing a finger to her chest. She was afraid. She got up again to leave.

"Quiet! Calm down." Ike tried to assuage her fears. "Sit down, I will explain everything."

"Me assist you to escape?" she lowered her voice. "Do you realize what you are saying?"

"Yes, you will assist me. I need you to assist me."

"You don't know what you are saying. I can't do that. You don't know my people."

"I don't, but you're the only one that can save my life. I know you have the will to set me free. I know you cannot allow me to die in this situation."

"Ikechukwu, this is hard to believe," the girl called his name in a familiar way. "Do you know what you are asking me to do?"

"I know. Be optimistic. *The pessimist sees the difficulty in every opportunity, the optimist sees the success.* Think positively. There's no doubt that we have a serious problem on our hands, but..."

"You and who?" the girl interrupted, her face grave.

Ike did not reply. Instead, he continued solemnly, "I know it is a serious matter, but, *like the hunter, we have to pursue the animal the way it runs.* I have no option. We have to follow this matter the way we see it. I don't have anybody to help me except you. I'm determined to get out of here alive, and we have to act quickly."

"You keep saying 'we,' who are 'we'?" Oliaku asked.

"You and I."

"Never! You must be mad. I'm a woman..."

"It doesn't matter? You don't have to fight. Women have special power. Women have accomplished great things. You're in and out of my jail. You're in a position to save my life if you want to. My hands and feet are swollen, I'm getting weaker everyday, and soon they will kill me. Oliaku I need your help. Set me free. Please help me."

Oliaku looked at Ike passionately. Her spirit sank into her belly at his appeal. Her heart melted when she noticed that Ike's eyes were glimmering with tears. She felt her own tears blurring her vision. She looked all over the prisoner, studying his bound hands and feet. They were swollen. She moved forward to the gate and peered to make sure no one was listening to their discussion. Everywhere was quiet as usual. She thought for a while and then gazed steadily at Ike.

"If I do this, my father will not waste a second to order my execution, do you know that?"

"Never! You won't be killed," Ike told her with an air of certainty.

She looked at Ike scornfully. "How do you know, do you know the King?"

"I tell you, nobody will harm you."

"You sound so stupid and ignorant," Oliaku rebutted. "You have no knowledge of the King?"

"I'll escape with you," Ike declared resolutely. "I can't leave you here. I'll take you with me."

"To your land?"

"Yes, to my land. I will go with you as soon as I'm set free."

Oliaku paused for a moment. He said he'd take me with him to his land, she thought.

It seemed she internalized this last statement. It even tickled her. But Ike's request left her confused. It appeared she needed help to make a decision.

In a thorny issue, Oliaku would solicit her mother's mature advice. But in this circumstance, her mother must not hear it, much less advising her positively. If her mother were to collaborate with them, if the plot leaked, her head would roll first before those of the plotters.

"Ike, I can't handle this," she said regretfully, looking at him with compassion.

"I believe you can," Ike encouraged. "You can if you are determined. You are the only human being in the world that can do this job. You know this. You are the only person that can save my life. And I believe you have the mind to make it happen."

"In as much as I don't want you to die..."

"If you don't want me to die," Ike interrupted her solicitously, "then save my life. I have done nothing to deserve this. I have never hurt a fly. I went to fish with my younger brother, it's an irony of fate that I'm trapped in this situation and will die if nobody reaches out to save my life. Help me."

Saying this, Ike's eyes loomed with tears again. He turned away his face and fought back the tears until they cleared. This is not the time to show weakness, he warned himself. Be a man, you must stretch your nerves to their limits. Women hate weak men, remember. If you want this girl to help you, avoid being emotional. Show that you can handle this task.

"If you don't want them to sacrifice me to their dead King, save my life. Save me from this unnecessary death," he pleaded.

The dialogue went on for a long time and then Oliaku's resistance began to crumble. Her wish to see Ike free became stronger. She had not accepted to do it, neither did she refuse. Ike was determined to win her full consent. There was no other way.

Heavily laden with this thorny issue, Oliaku suddenly hurried out of the barn, almost without excuse. She realized she had spent a lot of time in Ike's cell. Before she left, Ike warned her again never to tell anybody about their discussion. She promised not to tell anybody.

CHAPTER 18

In the night, Oliaku kept turning these things over in her mind. She couldn't sleep. She rolled from one end of her mat to another trying to figure out whether to consent to Ike's request or not. She was confused and afraid. She was almost certain that this was a suicidal undertaking.

Frustrated, and at a complete loss, she decided to reveal the matter to her mother contrary to what Ike told her. She thought perhaps her mother would help her make an informed decision. Oliaku had noticed how her mother waved her head pathetically the day she came into Ike's prison to check how her daughter was getting on with her assignments.

The woman had cast a compassionate look at Ike. Oliaku saw it. She also heard her mother say, under closed lips: "Oh, this is my fellow woman's child. Oh, poor thing." This in mind, Oliaku assumed her mother might have a negative view about Nzom's detestable culture.

Like the King, Oliaku's mother loved her daughter so much. She had never denied Oliaku any request. On matters requiring maternal advocacy, if Oliaku needed something she could not obtain by herself, the woman was apt to appeal to the King on Oliaku's behalf. Can mother be of help to me in this matter? Oliaku asked herself many times as the night wore on.

Oliaku shared her mother's hut. She was restless at her corner that night. Her mother had seen her go to her pouch which hung on the wall repeatedly. She had also gone out several times. Her mother became curious and asked Oliaku whether she was having bowel movement. Oliaku lied and said she was. It was at this point that the girl wanted to reveal what was weighing her down.

But on a second thought, she realized that this issue was not a simple domestic problem in which she could solicit her mother's help. This matter carried grave consequences - death. If a little mistake was made, she and her mother would be executed summarily. So she withheld her thoughts.

She went back to her mat pondering Ike's situation and the role she was required to play, but she couldn't arrive at a conclusion. She knew that in the morning, Ike would want to know what she had decided upon. She was, therefore, desperate to come up with a decision.

If things went wrong, she thought staring at her necklace hanging on the wall, my father will order his men to slaughter us like domestic animals. I know him. But if we succeeded, Ike said he'd take me to his land for safety. That sounds exciting, she speculated. But I'll miss my people.

Missing your people is not more important than the life of this young man, she challenged herself. After all you are a woman, and you'll some day leave home when you get married. Women are naturally transitory, from their biological homes to their new family home. So you'll invariably miss your people when you get married. That makes sense, she told herself.

Turning these options over and over in her mind, Oliaku did not know when she fell asleep. She hadn't slept for long when the cock crew, and it was the final cock-crow that heralded the day-break. Her mother woke her up, and she hurried to her morning duties.

When the prisoners' breakfast was ready, Oliaku went to Ike. The dialogue continued:

"Ike, I don't think I can do what you are asking me to do," she said innocently. "Sincerely, I don't think I can."

"You can," Ike assured her. "You have the courage, you have the will power, and you have the intelligence. You can, Oliaku," Ike called her name for the first time. "I believe you can."

To hear Ike mention her name, for the very first time, helped matter. It tickled her mind-set. It made a difference in her perception of this conspiracy. It infused a feeling of affection, encouraging and motivating her wavering spirit.

She cast a sympathetic look at the young man lying on the ground waiting to be sacrificed to the gods. She looked at his fascinating huge trunk. His face was sullen.

Oliaku thought: this handsome head will soon be severed from this huge trunk of a body and will be dumped into the grave side by side with King Udedibia's decomposed body. For what? she asked herself. What's the import of this ritual? Will the dead rise because of the sacrifice? Why should we bury the living with the dead? Why should the blood of this innocent man be shed? Why must this meaningless culture persist in our town? Why? Am I too young to understand the significance? Yes, it's our tradition; yes, it's the culture of the people; yes, our ancestors observed it; but why? What's the rationale? Is there any meaning attached to this rite that I did not know of? Mother could not explain this when I asked her. She does not know the meaning other than that 'it is to honor the dead'.

This is one of the senseless customs that our people perpetuate out of ignorance, Oliaku continued to criticize the ritual burial of her people. It should be discontinued. But who will tell them? Who can tell my people that this practice is inappropriate and barbaric? If I dare speak, I will be gone instantly. But I can still do something. I can tell my mother that this culture is stupid and absolutely unnecessary.

Oliaku was going through these thoughts when suddenly there was a commotion outside the compound. She wondered what was going on. She knew there was no event on the King's calendar. Not satisfied, she excused herself and ran to the gate.

She learned that the third man needed for the burial had been captured. The men were taking the captive into the palace. Women and children were kept out of it. The time for the funeral ceremony had come. The burial rites of the late King Udedibia Uyanne would now take place. This meant that Ike's time was up. Oliaku's spirit sank at this development.

According to the belief of the Nzom natives, the significance of human sacrifice was predicated on the premise that it would enable the spirit of the dead King to unite with the spirit of his ancestors. If the ritual was not accomplished, the man's spirit would be floating in the space because it did not possess the grits to mingle with the ancestors. The sacrifice, therefore, would give the people a sense of fulfillment; a feeling that the journey of the dead King to the ancestral realm was complete and that he was admitted and given a place among the gods. They also believed that if the ritual was not accomplished, the King's spirit would continue to haunt his children for life for failing to perform the sacrifice which was supposed to advance his course in the land of spirits.

When the noise died down, Oliaku came back to Ike looking dismal. Seeing her face, Ike new immediately that something was wrong. He looked at her inquiringly. Oliaku appeared reluctant to reveal what the commotion was all about. Instead, she gaped at Ike with a renewed feeling of empathy and compassion. She was contemplating how this man would be gone in a matter of hours and she would not see him any more. Her sudden change of mood triggered a wave of palpitation in Ike's heart. Oliaku could almost hear his heart drumming against his ribs.

"What is the noise about?" he asked Oliaku.

She turned away. Ike became suspicious. He knew that something had prompted this change of attitude. He wondered if they were coming to kill him. He began to feel that he might not survive this ordeal after all.

"Tell me, what is happening out there?" Ike urged Oliaku. He was anxious.

Oliaku looked at him sympathetically and sighed. She knew the news would devastate him and make him restless. After much pressure, she told Ike what the noise was about.

As Oliaku predicted, Ike was rattled to the marrow. "So the time has come," he said with trembling lips.

Oliaku did not speak. She stared at him with great concern.

Ike was worried. He looked above the trees in the barn. The birds were hopping on the branches in absolute freedom. He wished that these little creatures could descend and carry him to safety.

CHAPTER 19

Earlier, Ike had made up his mind that he was not going to die, but the latest news that the last man had been caught shattered all that was left of his hope to survive. Nevertheless, that hope and determination, resurfaced after the initial shock. His consternation took a reverse course and he looked less perturbed about his imminent death. His fears, which had reached a peak when Oliaku came in with the sad news, suddenly translated into a surge of energy. He looked at Oliaku and said,

"I'm not going to die."

"What!" Oliaku shouted, her face grave. She was more frightened than Ike.

"I must survive this ordeal," Ike vowed, "and this is the time for us to plan our escape. We have no time."

He continued to make the escape bid a dual package.

"Do you really want me to set you free Ike?" Oliaku asked, not clear about what to say or what to do at this critical moment.

"Definitely. I want you to save my life, please."

"Me?"

"Yes, you."

"This is a difficult task. I cannot handle it."

"I believe we can handle it," Ike assured her.

"I'll lose my life in a bid to save yours."

"Never! You won't lose your life. Nothing will happen to you. I'll protect you once I'm on my feet. I'll take you with me. They won't find you. If you set me free, I won't leave you behind. I promise. I'd rather die fighting to save your life than to see you die in their hands."

Oliaku looked at Ike with mixed feelings; feelings of compassion, fear, and enthusiasm. His courage in the face of danger was amazing. What a mettle! she thought.

"How can you do this?" she asked skeptically. "What are your strategies, seeing that your cell is heavily guarded by strong men?"

"All I need is your consent and cooperation. If I can count on your support, leave the rest to me. I can handle it. Once I'm on my feet, forget about how I'm going to take care of business."

Oliaku shook her head. She was rather impressed. She smiled at Ike's self-confidence. She was temporarily amused by his captivating poise. His courage was astonishing as well as intoxicating. She began to admire the heroism yet to be displayed by this man.

He must be a very strong man, she thought, probably a wrestler of the first class in his land. She studied his giant trunk at the turf and shook her head. She couldn't help adoring what she thought to be a tethered lion. She surveyed Ike's huge body lying helpless. She looked at his handsome face filled with desire; desire for freedom; desire for assistance; and desire to live. She looked at his broad chest, straying her eyes towards his hairy thighs, and then looked at his long hands both of which were swollen.

She was skeptical whether Ike could be able to fight in his present deteriorating condition. She wondered, should things went wrong, could he handle the squad of her father's tough men that had seen scores of tribal wars?

Judging from his age, Oliaku surmised, he hasn't seen any war. He may be a strong wrestler at his home, but *what can the stream do to the river, nor the rat do to an elephant?*

She looked at Ike adoringly. His entire structure was fascinating, cute, and fresh with his youthful age. Longingly, the girl fantasized seeing herself sitting on Ike's robust laps and rubbing a hand on his hairy chest. He must be a hero among his people, she thought. It's cruel to destroy this life.

Lost in this reverie, Oliaku suddenly realized the gravity of the situation at hand. She was aware that she was the only human being on earth that could help this man regain his freedom. Forthwith, her fears began to diminish. Her thoughts and feelings tilted towards seeking justification for Ike's freedom. In the conversation that followed, Ike observed that Oliaku was now leaning towards his objective.

His continuous pressure, coupled with his occasional bouts of tears had combined to muffle the girl's resistance. Gradually she became a willing tool. As her mind waxed stronger, she argued that there was no rationale in her people's ritual ceremony. She seemed to realize the impropriety and crudeness of the custom.

Her understanding of the worthlessness of the ritual gave birth to her decision to work with Ike for his freedom. Her morale became high as she got infected with Ike's personality and wooing strategies. Her heart was kindled with the zeal to see Ike regain his freedom. She wondered what Ike would look like when he stood on his feet. The desire to see him on his feet became another driving force.

"What are your plans?" she asked Ike on a serious note. "What do you intend to do, and what do you want me to do?"

Suddenly Oliaku lowered her voice and signaled Ike to do the same. She had spotted a movement towards the entrance of the barn. She fixed her eyes at the gate. A man's shadow showed up towards the door. Oliaku sprang to her feet and went to the door.

It was a member of the King's cabinet, Chief Nwasi Ikpeama, a tall figure with tribal marks. He was on a routine visit to ensure everything was okay. The King and his cabinet had spent a lot of time and resources to capture the men for the burial rites. They didn't want to loose any of them.

"I heard some voices in the barn," said the Chief truculently, his face tight and intimidating, "and I was wondering whom you were speaking with?"

His voice was perniciously threatening. His arid expression made Oliaku tremble. All members of the King's cabinet had prestigious stately clout that made people quiver. Chief Ikpeama had more of these qualities. His chieftaincy sway was frightening, and his imposing personality was arresting.

Oliaku's heart-beat increased at that question. She didn't expect it.

"Are you talking with him?" Chief Ikpeama demanded with a frightening look. "What were you saying to him?"

He leaned slightly on his walking stick and waited for an answer.

Oliaku's lips shivered as she searched for an answer. Fear contoured her lips but did not contour her cognitive capacity. She resented this man's presence, but she knew she must not talk to a cabinet chief in a disrespectful manner, even though she was the King's daughter. That should never happen. She controlled her anger and said:

"I was telling this man to eat. He had been refusing to eat."

"That's not an issue," the cabinet member snapped reproachfully, his face crimson. "Whether he eats or not, it doesn't make any difference at this point. His refusal to eat does not warrant any talking between you and him."

Satisfied that everything was normal, the man went away.

Oliaku watched him disappear towards the women's huts in the vast compound. "I hate this man", she said to her relief.

After that minor encounter, Oliaku's hatred on the culture of human sacrifice heightened. She was bitter about shedding innocent blood for the burial of a dead King who lived his full life span. If I had the power, she said to herself, I would abolish this tradition. It's crude, it's primitive, and it's pernicious.

At this point, Oliaku had made up her mind to swim or sink with Ike. She decided she must stop her people from performing this ritual even if it meant death for both of them. In the end, she resolved to do whatever Ike asked her to do.

She made the resolution in these words:

I must help this man to escape,
He'll take flight via our landscape,
I'll set him free, he must not die,
He is innocent, I hate to see him cry,
The wraths of the gods may visit me,
Their vengeance may come upon me,
Our fathers may revolt in their graves,
But surely, this man must be saved,
My ancestors may run riot with anger
They may even stab me with the dagger,
Their spleen may flow like the waves
But definitely this man must be saved
Let the world rumble and quake,
Let the heavens thunder and shake,
I must listen to Ike's tearful plea,
And I'm determined to set him free

CHAPTER 20

The arrangements for the funeral had geared up following the capture of the third man. Villages far and near had been informed about the new development. Dancing groups stepped up their preparations. It was going to be a remarkable event. Many people had never witnessed a ritual ceremony and were eager to see one. A lot more were just excited about the abundance of food and drinks. The King could afford a sumptuous meal for many.

Cows, oxen, sheep, and goats, littered King Uyanne's compound waiting to be slaughtered for the big feast. In addition, traditional rulers and clan heads from various towns and communities had donated goats and cattle to support King Uyanne. The best palm-wine tappers and brewers of local gin were instructed to channel all their daily production to the King's palace until the ceremony was over.

The King's compound had assumed a festive mood. Beginning from the day the third man was captured, the number of visitors in the palace had increased. Palm canopies and makeshift shelters were constructed in the open field to shelter the visitors.

Women were to cook food. Young men would assist with hewing the firewood and pounding cassava and yam-fofoo. Younger boys and girls would fetch water from the stream. Everybody had something to do.

Red cap chiefs from the thirteen villages in Nzom had been notified of the date. They were almost ready in their collective and individual preparations. The chiefs would be escorted to the King's house by their special dancing troupes. Their arrival would signal the commencement of the event.

In the evening when Oliaku came to feed Ike, her face was somber. She looked worried.

"Now Ike, you must do whatever you want to do to save your life," she said, almost in tears, "These people will reach for your head in less than two days."

Ike looked awful. He stared at Oliaku hopelessly. "Is that right?"

"Yes. Visitors are now pouring into the palace."

"Hmmm!" Ike sighed.

Oliaku looked at him pathetically focusing particularly on his swollen hands and feet. The rope had almost eaten into his flesh and his skin was beginning to peel.

Can this man walk with these feet, let alone run with them? Oliaku asked herself. They are in bad shape. Should things get out of hand, how can he function with these weak limbs that have not been used for a while? What are we going to do? Is this not a suicidal bid?

Whom shall I ask to help me? A dangerous undertaking such as this requires the intervention of the gods. I would've asked the ancestors to come to my aid, but the ritual is in their favour and I'm working against it, how can they support me? Who fights against self? It's obvious that their anger is hot against me and their swords are pointed to my heart. How can they support me? But I have a duty to perform. I must save this man, let the gods rage.

After these reflections, Oliaku was motivated. Her determination was actuated by her thoughts. She had made up her mind to deliver Ike from the hands of her people. The question was no longer: whether she would participate in the plan? The issue now was: what part she was going to play? She wanted to know.

The girl waited for directives from Ike. She was prepared to help in any way he wanted. The acceptance of the challenge was written on her face; it was seen in her actions; and reflective in her speech. Ike had no problem discerning this. He was happy that he could now count on Oliaku's full support.

Ike had only two days to live. He was disconcerted, but inside, his spirit was high. Despite the seriousness of the situation, he emitted placidity, collectedness, and poise. He was keyed up by Oliaku being anxious to see this scheme started immediately. He knew that the hour of his salvation had come, and he must act quickly.

"Have you made up your mind to help me?" he asked Oliaku.

"Yes," she replied promptly.

She bent down and brushed some dirt off Ike's hairy chest, and tidied his face in a most affectionate and maternal fashion.

"Well then, let's get to work. We have no time to waste. I thank you for consenting to help me. It's a big sacrifice which only a few can make. You are indeed a brave woman. Your courage has energized my spirit and I'm determined to save our lives. If you save my life, I'll pay you back."

Ike sighed heavily and went on: "The first thing I want you to do is this: tomorrow afternoon, go to the bush and pluck some medicinal leaves – *ulodu, uturukpa, nwanju, and waliwa*. Are you familiar with these herbs?"

"Sure, my grandmother was a herbalist," Oliaku replied and looked at Ike inquiringly. "What do you want to do with these?"

"In the evening preceding the fateful day, squeeze the leaves thoroughly and drop the juices in the food you serve the guards for supper. Can you do this?"

"It is simple," Oliaku replied humbly, "I serve their meals. Why the poison? Do you want to kill all my people?"

'It's part of the plan," Ike replied. "The herbs won't kill them."

"And why do you want to involve other guards?

"I want us to help all the prisoners to escape. They don't deserve to die."

Oliaku was taken aback. "Why do you want to save others when you have not saved yourself?" she asked. "Why don't you concentrate on your safety?"

Ike paused for a moment. "Listen, if things worked out well, if we had the time, we could help them escape too. I don't want them to die. Just do as I say, everything will be fine, trust me.

"Now, listen carefully. As soon as you serve the guards their supper, know that in a short time, the herbs in their meal will put them to sleep. The herbs have strong sedating compound. At this point, know that the operation has started.

"Keep watch, when the guards have fallen asleep, set me free and we shall go to other prisoners to set them free. Do you follow what I'm saying?"

Oliaku's face showed skepticism. "Are you sure this plan will work?"

"Hopefully."

"What is your contingency arrangement should things go contrary to your expectations?"

"Good question. All I want is to be set free. Once I am on my feet, leave the rest to me."

Oliaku looked at Ike admiringly. She adored his bravery. His mettle dazzled her imagination.

"Once I'm on my feet, the job is as good as accomplished. I don't care if I have a dozen men to deal with. Just play your part and leave the rest to me. The dog says: *Just drop the bone out there, don't worry about my struggle for possession with the spirits.*"

"Ha-ha-ha!" Oliaku laughed almost aloud. But when Ike looked at her disapprovingly she cupped her mouth.

"Remember what is at stake," he reprimanded her politely. "If they see you laughing in my confinement, they will suspect something?"

"Don't worry, I can always find an excuse," Oliaku replied apologetically. "I did so when Chief Ikpeama caught us talking, remember?"

"We must be careful. This is the only chance we have, and we must not blow it. Any mistake will cost us dearly. We have plenty of time to revel if we succeed. But for now, let's be serious."

"Ike, do you think we will come out alive after this?"

"Yes."

Oliaku was afraid. Somehow, Ike's warning made her realize the risk involved in this venture. Often her mood swung from better to worse, and from worse to fair.

Ike reassured her. "I'm positive we'll succeed. All I need is your cooperation.

If your heart is as strong as mine, we shall make it. I'll take care of everything when the time comes."

"Ike, my fear is that your hands and legs are feeble. You've been lying here for days. Can you function effectively on these swollen limbs? Aren't they painful?"

"I can stand any force, trust me. All I need is your support. Don't shake in your will. Be resolute and execute your part of the scheme with precision. Don't make mistakes and don't waste time.

"I believe you're a brave man, full of courage and determination," Oliaku said, delighted at Ike's confidence. "I feel as though we have already succeeded."

"When your life is at stake," Ike said shrewdly, "you have no choice but to strive to survive?"

Oliaku felt heart-broken. She looked at Ike sympathetically and hissed. She came closer, knelt beside him and examined his swollen legs. "Are you sure you can run with these bad legs?"

"Yes."

"I'll set you free tomorrow night, even if it means my death. I stand to die with you. I must help you regain your freedom. I'll give you every support you needed to return to your people. My heart is strong, and my spirit is willing"

As Oliaku spoke, she stroked at Ike's chest unconsciously, pulling gently on the hair.

"Your courage has energized my spirit," she continued, "I'm ready for action. We're fighting against an obnoxious culture, and we must triumph."

Ike was glad. Oliaku's comments raised his spirit. "Yes, dear," he said, "we're fighting against a crude tradition, and we must triumph. I admire your bravery. One more thing, and we will be done with this plan."

Oliaku smiled, adjusted her sitting position, and listened attentively. She was almost leaning lovingly on Ike's body.

"If you have any valuables, like clothing or something you would like to take with you, put them together and hide them in a secret place where it can be reached at a glance. Do you understand?"

"Yes. I'm excited," she said enthusiastically.

Ike looked at her confused. "Excited about what?"

"Excited about this whole business."

"Do you understand what you're saying? Do you realize what we are in for?"

"I do."

"What is exciting about a do-or-die undertaking?"

"I just want to see it happen. I want to see you free. I want you to reunite with your people and you'll introduce me to them."

Ike shook his head. "Childishness."

CHAPTER 21

The funeral of late King Udedibia Uyanne was only a day away. Arrangements were almost complete. The three men needed for the burial were in the King's dungeon waiting to be beheaded. The quantity of food and drinks in the store were abundant. The animals - cows, goats, sheep, and horses for the celebration were plentiful. Everything was set.

A well known clairvoyant who would officiate in the ritual ceremony had arrived with his oracle. He would lead the people through the process of human sacrifice. He would chant incantations during the oblation. And then he'd slash the throats of the victims, pour their blood in the grave, and deposit their heads down his feet. The man had been conferring with the King in his chamber.

"Get the heads of the men thoroughly shaven," the medium instructed the King. "After that, rub "*Nzo*" (white chalk) on their heads and on their eyelashes. Prepare a good meal and give them the best part, the best meat, and the best wine, as much as they want."

"It will be done as you said," King Uyanne replied.

Mediums and seers commanded great respect among the people. Even the Kings seek and obey their advice.

Visitors had started arriving at the King's palace in large numbers. Some dancing groups had arrived. The most famous masquerades in the area, *Agaba, Omaba, Nwangwu-Igbakwu*, and *Akuebilisi*, had started arriving in the palace. Entertainment troupes were allotted spots in the huge compound as they arrived.

The atmosphere was clad in colorful festivity. Echoes of drums reverberated from the distance. Unless you were close to a dancing group, you could hardly distinguish the rhythm of one drum from another. People in ceremonial mood streamed into the compound continuously.

Although people were many in the King's palace the real ceremony was yet to begin. Every now and then a red cap Chief, dressed in his magnificent chieftaincy regalia, walked across the field, waving his ox-tail insignia and acknowledging people's greetings. This added glamour to the occasion.

Every now and then, a masquerade stirred the crowd, causing women and children to stampede. This was a thrilling aspect of the event. Tomorrow would be the big day. The prisoners would be sacrificed and buried with the dead King Udedibia. Everybody knew about the big feast and the funeral, but few knew about the ritual.

Busy working in her mother's hut, Oliaku wasn't unaware of the events galore outside. She heard all the hullabaloos in the palace. She was handling two major functions - her official duties in the palace and her assignments for Ike's escape. Somehow, *she was running with the hare and chasing with the hound.*

To satisfy her curiosity, occasionally, she peeped outside to get a glimpse of what was going on. And then she'd rush back to her assignments. Her mind was not at rest. She was still skeptical about the secret business. She kept wondering whether the plan would succeed. But she had made up her mind to assist Ike irrespective of what the outcome was going to be.

Following Ike's instructions, Oliaku had put together her personal belongings in readiness for their flight. She hid the parcel where no one could see it, and where she could reach it at the neck of time. She did not forget to get her necklace, her most prized possession. The man who gave her the necklace was her fiancé who was to marry her in the next few months. The ornament was very expensive. She wore it only during big festivals such as the funeral ceremony going on. She did not regret leaving Aneke behind because she didn't even like him. He was an old man, but the King insisted she must marry Aneke because he was an influential traditional ruler.

Earlier in the day, Oliaku had plucked the leaves as Ike instructed her. In order to make sure the herbs were the correct ones, she took them to Ike for confirmation. They couldn't afford to make any mistake. Ike examined the leaves one by one.

"They are fine," he announced. "They are the correct species."

"Are you sure?" Oliaku asked. She wanted to be 100% sure.

"Yes. They are the right ones."

As the King and his household were putting finishing touches to the preparation for tomorrow's ritual killing, his daughter, Oliaku, and one of the captives, were busy planning the escape of the three prisoners held in the cell for the ritual sacrifice.

Is this plan going to succeed? Oliaku asked herself. Are we going to make it? What have we forgotten to put in place? Oh, our fathers, help us in this deadly venture.

You cannot invoke your dead fathers in this circumstance, she reminded herself. You are working against their wish, remember. They cannot help you. Instead, they will curse you. They will wage a war against you for trying to disrupt the ritual ceremony meant for their wellbeing. Their retribution will descend on you instead.

Oliaku paused and weighed these thoughts. Whatever, she sighed. She became afraid. Will the gods actually work against me? she asked herself. But there are good gods who would not like innocent blood to be shed? May these good gods lend me their hands.

She was entertaining some fears - genuine fears. She knew that the failure of their venture would spell doom for both of them. Her father would order her instant execution, and they would still slaughter Ike for the ritual ceremony. Nevertheless, the girl had made up her mind to do it.

On his part, Ike was resolute. Starting from the day Oliaku consented to set him free, he had prepared his mind for a showdown. For him, it was a do-or-die escapade. He had no choice. In preparation for the risky affair, he kept stretching his hands and legs to enliven the vapid limbs and to promote the flow of blood down the extremities.

A few days ago, at his request, Oliaku had slackened the ropes to permit blood flow. She did it so cleverly that nobody would notice any change in the original structure of the tether. This gave Ike a lot of relief. His swollen feet had started going down, and he was gaining strength on both legs. Inside, he felt vibrant. The wound on his shoulder had since healed and there was no pain from that sector. Oliaku purposely gave Ike double ration everyday to compensate for the lost muscle power, beef up his physical strength; and make him feel healthier and stronger.

CHAPTER 22

Finally the big day came. At lunch, Oliaku fed Ike very well and he was steaming with vigor. He was bubbling with stamina and was ready for action at night-fall. He asked Oliaku questions about the physical locations of houses and the direction of the main entrance gate. He needed this information in case of emergency during their escape. He was taken to Umuiwu blindfolded, and he had not seen the light of day since then.

"Since we shall be escaping with other prisoners," Oliaku said, "shall I go and whisper to them about this arrangement so they can get prepared for the flight?"

"No," Ike replied abruptly. "Don't let anybody know this. Only you and I should know about this plan. If another ear hears it, we are doomed. When we set them free, we will give them the situation instruction and they will be pleased to flee with us. Every creature runs when its life is threatened. The only living thing that does not run is tree."

"Ike, suppose they move you to a place where I cannot see you before we strike?" Oliaku asked, intelligently. She was filled with consternation. Her heart was beginning to pulsate.

Ike looked up in search of an answer. He wanted to scratch his head, but his hands were held by the ropes. "Well, if they take me away before midnight, that's it. I will die. But at least you have tried. I'll always remember you wherever I am. I'll always remember that you tried your best to save my life. I can't forget you even at death. I can't forget your kindness and care for me."

Oliaku's eyes became wet as Ike expressed his appreciation for her efforts. She undid one end of her wrapper and wiped her tears. Ike became emotional too, but he tried to suffocate his tears. In a masculine note, he told Oliaku that *the war box is not concerned with sentiment*, and that she must wipe her tears and focus attention on the plan.

"God forbid, you won't die," Oliaku said in a trembling tone. "I'll save you. I'll set you free. Anywhere they take you to, I will come there and set you free. I'll follow them till I fulfill this goal. I hate these brutes."

"Be watchful from now on," Ike told her prudently. "Check every movement. Listen to every conversation and every whisper. Monitor every proceeding of the funeral arrangements. Be on alert, so they don't take us unaware. Any time you notice that the King and his council are in consultation, find out what the discussion is about and let me know immediately. Watch everybody, especially the guards, but be careful not to wear a suspicious look that might betray your heart's content. Act as if nothing is going on. Go about your normal business. Be observant and be as wise as the serpent.

"Listen," Ike continued on a very serious note. Oliaku looked at him obsequiously, her arms wrapped around her midsection in utter consternation. She had never seen Ike look more serious and tense. "I think they are likely to kill us (the captives) in the early hours of the morning, this is what I think. I may be wrong."

"Yes, I heard my mother say that the execution will be at the third cock-crow, just before dawn."

"Good. I'm glad we now know the time. All the same, we cannot take anything for granted. Any time you notice unusual movements, or you suspect that the men are gathering together, don't hesitate to rush in here to pass words to me. This is very important. Stand on your toes from now on.

"If they didn't pre-empt our plan, we will strike in the middle of the night when everybody is asleep."

"Ike nobody is going to sleep tonight," Oliaku said predictively. "I have seen many big ceremonies. People are usually awake dancing and drinking till the next morning. Don't expect that they will ever go to sleep tonight. Never! The activities will continue till the crack of dawn."

"In a way, that will be advantageous for our purpose," Ike replied thoughtfully. If there happens to be any commotion as we execute our plan, the music and merry-making will drown the noise. This will facilitate our course."

"Are you saying that the sound of drums will swallow any noise our action might generate?" Oliaku asked.

"Exactly."

"That makes sense," Oliaku nodded her head.

The zero hour had come. Fear had suddenly gripped her. The enthusiasm with which she greeted this proposal earlier had disappeared. Her face looked grim and cheerless. Her heart-beat increased. Ike could almost hear her heart thumping.

"Are you afraid"? he asked with concern.

"No," Oliaku lied.

"But you look worried?"

"I'm fine. I'm only concerned about what will happen if we fail."

"Don't waiver, we're going to make it. I'm optimistic we shall succeed."

"Do you think so?" Oliaku asked with mixed feelings.

"Trust me. We shall make it. We can't fail."

"What makes you think so?' Oliaku insisted with a flicker of hope resurging in her. Her face was beginning to radiate with renewed zeal.

"My mind tells me that we shall be successful in this enterprise," Ike replied firmly. "But don't let us waste time on reviewing success and failure. Let's get to work and retouch our plans. The dusk is gathering. And once it is dark, you don't know when they will come to get me."

"Ike, are you sure we are not *weaving a rope of sand here?"* Oliaku asked, as she regained her confidence.

"No. We are *weaving a rope of tough pine,"* he replied.

As if by magic, that reassurance from Ike boosted her sagging spirit. She bounced back to life and began to act vivaciously as before. Together they continued to rehearse and polish the blueprint of their hazardous experiment. Together they modeled and remodeled their strategies until they were satisfied that every tiny hole had been plugged.

Night seemed to drag its feet, so it seemed to Oliaku, as she looked forward to the midnight when the operation would commence. She wanted everything to come to pass. Above all, her preoccupation was to see this man stand on his two legs a free man. She couldn't wait.

She moved around watching every movement, surveying all corners, monitoring the guards in their posts, assessing their mood, checking and rechecking everything as Ike instructed her. Alert, with the sensitivity of a cat, Oliaku even looked at shadows twice.

Any time she noticed a suspicious movement, she sneaked into the barn and briefed Ike, and would receive fresh instructions. Her eyes were as sharp as the hawk's. She was indeed fit for this task. No one would believe that this was the, hitherto, an inane, ignorant, and rustic damsel that knew nothing. The little coaching Ike gave her had revolutionized her intellectual capability. A shrewd accomplice with great intuition, Oliaku was performing this function with astounding accuracy. While she attended to her assignments in the palace, she rehearsed her plot with Ike inwardly.

Out in the compound, people were busy drinking and dancing. As the night wore on, children began to retire to their mother's huts. Some women too were retiring. Tired and drunken guests were sprawling at all corners. But a large number of celebrants were still moving around in different directions. Music groups and drummers were still on. The palace was alive with colourful traditional entertainments. Distant villagers heard the drums loud and clear. People enjoyed themselves. Food and drinks were surplus.

King Udedibia's death was a great ceremony. During his lifetime, he traveled far and wide. He made friends and foes alike. He fought many tribal wars. His fame knew no boundary. That was why his burial attracted so many people. That was why his people considered it imperative and obligatory to bury him with human heads. The Nzom people believed their King deserved ritual interment.

CHAPTER 23

As Oliaku moved around the courtyard, she became concerned about the incessant traffic of people. She went to Ike and said, "I'm afraid the human traffic in the palace is disturbing. "Do you think we can accomplish our objective without being observed?"

"Yes, if we are careful," Ike replied. "I think that the movement of people will not interfere with our plan because the rowdy atmosphere will provide cover for our purpose. People will focus their attention on festive activities. As soon as you set me free we will find our way out."

After each instruction and reassurance, Oliaku bounced back to vivacity. She told Ike that she was not afraid of anything and that her eagerness to see him on his feet transcended all fears.

Finally, the hour came. It was almost midnight. The first cockcrow from the distance signaled the middle of the night. Oliaku was keeping time and keeping watch.

Till today, cockcrow remains a mechanism for time-keeping among the rural dwellers in Africa and most other parts of the world. While they use cockcrow in the night, they use the sun in the day to keep the time. When the shadow is squatty, they know it is around midday. When it becomes elongated, they know the dusk is gathering. Although clocks are available today, for most villagers, the cockcrow and the sun remain significant in the mode of time-keeping for rural folks.

Oliaku applied this art effectively this night. As soon as she heard the first cockcrow from the distance, she moved surreptitiously to the King's private chamber.

Only the King and his top messengers had access to this special department of the King's chamber. Oliaku had the privilege to go there. In the chamber, Oliaku pulled a two edged sword which was the King's special war arsenal. Nobody, except the King, used this sword. The blade was incredibly sharp and could sever a human throat with the strike of a child.

In his lifetime, late King Udedibia Uyanne used this sword to fight tribal wars. He bequeathed it to his son, King Ekwealor Uyanne, who had used it in some local wars.

After securing the weapon, Oliaku hid it in her waist-cloth and tiptoed into the darkness. Nobody saw her. Even if they saw her, there was no cause for alarm for she had access to all parts of the King's private places.

The drums and dancing were in progress, but there was a reduction of noise and uproar resonating from the castle as people fell asleep in their chairs. Some visitors and guests spread their clothes on the ground and lay on them. Those who came with their mats had the luxury of comfortable sleeping arrangements.

Men were still drinking. Drunkards could be heard shouting on top of their voices, cursing and swearing at one another.

"Give us more drinks!" they demanded, even though they had surplus at their disposal.

Clutching the sword securely, Oliaku hurried straight to the barn where Ike was waiting. At the gate, she saw the guard sleeping. The man was supposed to be awake. The poison had taken effect.

Ike was waiting anxiously for her. They must start immediately or else the executioners would arrive any time to take him away.

"Ike," Oliaku whispered in the dark. "I'm here."

"Good," Ike responded lively, "you came at the right time. I just heard the first cock-crow a moment ago and I felt this was the time. Did anybody see you?"

"No." Oliaku replied.

"Are you ready?"

"Yes."

"Are you afraid?"

"No. I rely on your wisdom and your strength. Anything you want me to do, I'll do it for you."

"Now, don't make mistakes. Do whatever I tell you to do. Did you put the herbs in the guards' food?"

"Yes. They have all fallen asleep."

"Good. This is the time. Don't fear. Don't waiver. You are a brave girl. Word cannot express your gallantry and fortitude. I won't disappoint you. Once I am on my feet, you'll realize what I have been telling you. This is the procedure, as soon as I'm on my feet, take me to other captives. Should there be a struggle between me and the guards during the operation, don't panic, don't scream in despair. Just do all you can to assist me. But always keep away from danger. Watch my movements and be close enough to escape with me when I'm ready to retreat. Remember that I do not know the way around the castle, worse still, it is night. Chances are that I might scamper into the enemy location while trying to escape."

CHAPTER 24

Oliaku swung into action with her knife. In the darkness of the barn, she ripped off the rope that held Ike. Ike was free. He sprang up like a leopard and threw his hands around Oliaku and lifted her up in the air with deep affection. He kissed her most passionately. He knelt down and kissed her feet. Goose bumps bathed Oliaku's body as Ike demonstrated his gratitude and genuine affection. Nobody had treated her so reverently.

"Ah-a, I'm free!" Ike said in a low tone as he stretched his feeble limbs to restore strength and vitality.

Oliaku surveyed Ike in the darkness. He towered above like a giant. He had a huge trunk, broad shoulders, and stout muscles. He was huge, more than Oliaku had thought. Oliaku had never seen such an oversized man. Looking at his image now that he was on his feet, Oliaku became terrified of the man she had watched lying on the ground helpless.

Ike radiated astounding valour and unimaginable magnetism. Without wasting a second he signaled Oliaku to lead the way to the other cells. He moved sharply with heroism behind her. Outside the gate Ike and Oliaku heard some voices approaching their direction. They retreated into the barn. Ike grabbed the sword from Oliaku and poised for action. He thought they were coming to get him.

Fear gripped Oliaku again. She lost her breath and was trembling. But Ike reassured her. He was already in a fighting mood. He was prepared for anything now that he was on his feet. His eyes emitted fire.

I would prefer to die fighting than having my throat slashed without resistance, Ike told himself as he and Oliaku waited for the executioners to enter the barn. Oliaku was even restraining him from bursting outside the barn to cut them down.

The voices were not those of the executioners after all. They faded away towards the bush.

"The men went to the nearby shrubs," Oliaku whispered to Ike, "most probably to ease themselves."

When the voices had died down completely, Ike and Oliaku emerged from the barn. Ike saw his guard deep in sleep at the door. He picked up the man's sword. Oliaku led him to the confinement of the other two captives.

First, they went to Adrika's cell, the first prisoner. Adrika's guard was fast asleep under the influence of the drug that Oliaku had put in his meal.

Cautiously they sneaked into the barn walking on their toes and freed Adrika. This time Ike did the job of cutting the ropes while Oliaku kept watch. Adrika was taken aback. Have they come to kill me? he thought. He rubbed his eyes to ensure it wasn't a dream. It was real.

He was confused. The cell was dark but he could see two figures, a man and a woman. He was able to recognize Oliaku who came often to feed him, but the man, he did not know.

Adrika was aware that he was going to be sacrificed to the gods. Oliaku had told him. "It's time," he thought.

With a finger in his mouth, Ike signaled to Adrika to seal his lips. "You're being rescued," he whispered to Adrika, "say nothing at all, just follow behind us and do what you're told."

Adrika managed to stand on his feeble legs but could hardly walk. His legs were stiff. He tried to force them but the legs would not comply easily. They had been stationary and had become lethargic. This might jeopardize the operation. Ike and Oliaku did not take this into account during their plan.

Although his legs did not want to comply, Adrika forced them to move and they began to respond. He limped behind Ike and Oliaku, gaining some strength as he did. In no time, blood began to circulate down his extremities. He felt better. He could even run.

There was no time to waste. Adrika became aware he was at the verge of regaining his freedom. He was so happy even though they were not yet out of the woods.

Again the party tiptoed to the next cell. As they moved, they seized weapons from the sleeping guards. Adrika had regained enough strength to fight.

Tragedy!

When Ike and his team approached the third barn, alas! the guard was awake.

"Heavens!" Ike shouted under his breath. "This one is awake."

Oliaku was frozen. Fear gripped her to the bones. She shivered. But Ike reassured her. They stood afar in the darkness and watched the guard. He was sitting at the entrance of the barn snuffing. His small lantern was glowing in the murky night. His weapon was at his side.

A chill ran through Oliaku's spine. She began to tremble with fear. She almost screamed for she thought this was the end of the mission. The three of them would be picked up and butchered. Ike ordered a retreat. He advised Oliaku to step away. He had noticed how the girl was shaking.

Even if they decided not to rescue the third man, they would still pass across this barn. There was no other way. Their escape route lay across this barn and the guard was sitting there. They must get rid of him before they could get across. The King's palace was well fortified.

"Why is he awake?" Ike whispered to Oliaku at a safe distance. "Did he not eat the dinner?"

"I'm sure I smeared his soup with the herbs as I did others'." Oliaku defended herself.

"Did he not eat it?" Ike asked puzzled.

"He probably did not," Oliaku replied in a trembling voice.

At first Adrika was confused about what was going on. The only thing clear to him was that they were trying to escape. But soon he realized that they were attempting to rescue the third prisoner like he was rescued. He followed behind Ike with his knife ready. His legs were now strong enough to put up a reasonable fight if need be.

Ike thought for a moment and signaled the rest of the party to wait in the dark. He tiptoed towards the edge of the fence unobtrusively, and then detoured via the eastern side of the courtyard taking care not to be noticed by the guard or anybody else. He then trailed from behind stepping cautiously not to rustle dry leaves that might attract attention. He kept a slow surreptitious movement till he closed in on the guard.

In a flash, he dived forward and grabbed the guard by the throat choking him.

A fierce struggle ensued. The man was equally huge and robust. Ike held the man down with his strong hands so tight that it was amazing how heroically and successfully he could do that. Instantly, Oliaku and Adrika rushed out to assist him.

While Ike was holding the guard firmly by the mouth with both hands, Adrika ran his sword into the man's heart. He dropped on the ground without a scream.

Oliaku was terrified at the ensuing fight. She never expected this. She was equally amazed at Ike's prowess and natural stamina. She trembled in fear. Her whole being shook convulsively. Ike reassured her, and warned her to get herself together.

"You must be brave," Ike whispered to her. "We need to do this in order to save our lives. Be courageous, I'm in control."

Oliaku did not expect there would be any bloodshed, nor did Ike. They had planned to set all the prisoners free and then to tiptoe out of the place without any struggle. But the situation turned out differently. Ike had asked Adrika to strike, and he did. *If the music changes, the*

dancers change style. If the fact changes, the strategy is altered.
These were Ike's thoughts following this development. He
was prepared for any unexpected outcome. Therefore, in
order to save their lives, a head had to roll.

Quickly they released Ogugua, the third prisoner.
He was a promising young man like Ike. Ogugua was
even awake when they came to him. The commotion
had awakened him and he seemed to realize what was
going on. In a lowered tone, the leader of the rescue party
briefed him about their intention. Ogugua was delighted
to regain his liberty. He was only a few days in captivity,
so he was still strong and vivacious.

Ogugua leapt unto his feet as if nothing had happened
to his legs. He armed himself with one of the swords and
waited for an order from the leader of their revolution.
Oliaku announced under her breath that they must hurry
towards the back of the small hut sheltering the King's
oracle. This route would take them out of the palace
through the back door. She led the way.

But alas! another tragedy. They had been spotted.
Some armed men were coming.

"Good gracious!" Ike screamed. "Lord have mercy!"

"Nnemoooo!" Oliaku cried. "We're finished."

Ike and his men realized at this moment that they
were in danger. They had been spotted. Confusion.

Earlier when the scuffle between Ike and the dead
guard was going on, Oliaku had seen an elderly man
emerged from the house and proceeded to the nearby
bush to urinate. The man probably saw the struggle and
became suspicious. Suspecting that some drunken men

were fighting, the man alerted the King's security. Oliaku did not realize that the man had seen them.

Four men were running towards the scene with their swords drawn.

"Ike run...run...run!" Oliaku shouted. "Save your life, they are coming...they are coming! Run, run, run!"

Before Ike and the two prisoners could take flight, the men were already on them.

Horror! The music and the entertainment were going on in the palace. People did not know what was happening.

Oliaku was frozen. The mission has failed! she cried in her heart, "Ohooooooo!"

There was no way to escape now. They had no alternative but to face the men in combat. This was a suicidal venture, three against four. Ike didn't expect his plan would turn into this nightmarish chaos.

Oliaku retreated to the gate and stood panicking and crying. She knew they would lose the battle because she believed that the weak prisoners were no match to the strong warriors that protected the King. Standing away in the dark, she wept. She wondered why she had to go into this. She blamed herself for the step she had taken.

Her feet became numb. Her heart was pounding at a speed in which breathing became difficult. She began to regret her action in releasing the King's captives billed for funeral sacrifice. There's no doubt, my death is near, she thought. Ooooh Ike! Even if the guards spared my life after killing the prisoners, the King must order my execution for my involvement in this. This is the end of my life.

But in her heart, Oliaku felt satisfied for setting Ike free. At least she fulfilled her promise. But she was afraid to die for doing so.

Ike was in front of the escapees. Suddenly, one of the guards charged towards him with his sword raised. But with an agile movement, Ike leapt aside like a cat avoiding a fatal blow. He followed up with a quick stab to the assailant's stomach. The man's intestines gushed out. He gasped and fell. Ike's sword almost came through his back.

Seeing that their leader had fallen, fear gripped the men. Ike charged again with a dazzling movement at another man.

In the disorderly mayhem, one of the King's men engaged Adrika in a blow for blow combat. Adrika fought bravely but couldn't sustain much longer. However, before he was brought down, he had inflicted a deep cut into his attacker's forehead. Both he and the man fell.

Ike was left with Ogugua. Ogugua was looking vivacious. He was as young as Ike and equally a brave warrior. In fact Ogugua was a hero in his native land. He had fought a tribal war and had some experience.

Despite the fact that they were frail as a result of their incarceration, both men fought gallantly. Ogugua had earlier grounded one man, but paid the price with a cut on his left shoulder. However, it wasn't a fatal cut.

Ike was still fighting fiercely. He had grounded one man. Adrika had killed one man before he was brought down. Ogugua got one man. This left their opponents with one man.

Seeing he was alone, the fourth man attempted a retreat, but Ike foiled that attempt. He rushed at him and gave him a dastard machete-cut at the nape. The man fell backwards.

Without wasting time, Ike and Ogugua retreated into the darkness where Oliaku was waiting and fighting her own battle in her heart. She couldn't believe what she saw - **victory.** Before the guards could reorganize, Ike, Ogugua, and Oliaku had fled in the darkness. They were victorious, but they lost Adrika.

CHAPTER 25

The head of the King's guard was alarmed at what had happened. Fearing that the King might execute him and his men, he immediately detailed twenty hefty warriors to pursue the escapees and to bring them back. "Your life and mine depend on the success of your mission," he told the emissaries. "You must bring these men back tonight or else the King will slay everybody before the day-break.

Armed to the teeth, the warriors raced off to recapture Ike and his team.

Meanwhile, after escaping from the battle scene, Ike, Oliaku, and Ogugua had began a long journey to Ifite. They traversed the vast landscape of the Nzom territory in the dead of the night running as fast as they could. Oliaku was leading the way because she knew the environment more than any member of the escapees. However, it's most likely that when they entered the outskirt of the town, where there were no houses to provide landmarks, her knowledge of the Nzom landscape would be put to test.

Soon the speculation became real. Oliaku was no longer able to pilot the journey. Her cognitive map of Nzom's topography at the outskirt of the town was not sharp enough to direct the path leading to safety; and it was dark too. The escapees were stuck. This was not a good omen.

At this juncture, Ike realized that their problem was not yet over. He cautioned carefulness in their next move or else they would end up wandering back into the enemy land. He was yet speaking when suddenly there came faint thudding of footsteps from the distance. They stopped and listened. The tramping became louder and louder, coming quickly behind them. They suspected that some people were approaching their direction.

Quickly, Ike signaled Oliaku and Ogugua to retreat into the bush. The pounding of footsteps increased in intensity followed by bouts of "Hm! Hm! Hm!" like the men in a battle mood. Ike whispered another instruction. They dived into the interior of the forest.

Oliaku's heart started pounding again. She began to cry. She had thought that their problem was over. "So all we had suffered to get here was in vain," she whispered impetuously. "These men are from the palace. They are after us. They can search this forest and find us. Ohooooo my life!"

She felt her world crashing again. She suspected that the King had ordered his men to recapture them. She believed that if the men spread out in the forest they could flush them out and take them away.

Ike remained unabashed. He reassured her, "We will be okay. They will not find us. We must get back home even if it means another fight."

His bravado notwithstanding, Oliaku said in her heart, *the stream constitutes no danger to the river.*

Soon the warriors raced up and passed the escapees' hiding position. Although it was dark, the escapees could see the men with their weapons raised up. At this point, Ike and his team were convinced that the King's men were looking for them.

For hours, they did not move in their hiding place while the emissaries searched the environment.

When they heard the third cock-crow from a distant village, they knew that day-break was imminent. They began to prepare for the worst, not knowing whether the warriors were lying in wait or gone. They armed themselves with the weapons they recovered from Nzom and began to creep out of the jungle surreptitiously. It was difficult to tell if the warriors were still searching the forest. Ike was prepared for anything. He could fight again if necessary.

Soon it was day-break, and Ike was leading the way out of the jungle. He surveyed the surroundings. There was nobody. He assumed that the Nzom men had gone back to their land. The escapees began to hurry home. The next village was only a few miles away and they would leave Nzom behind.

They travelled a long way and soon arrived at Obe, a neighbouring village to Nzom. They were almost sure of safety in Obe, but none of them wanted to give anything to chance, so they continued running. After Obe, the escapees would have to travel across seven more towns and villages before reaching Ifite land.

From Obe Ike had taken the lead. He knew how to get to Ifite from there. They travelled a long way without resting. Eventually they entered Ifite forest. They were all tired, famished, but overjoyed. They felt secured when they walked into the Ifite farmland. Some farmers were already in their farms working.

Suddenly an Ifite farmer who knew Ike caught sight of him and took to her heels crying and screaming. She thought she had seen a ghost, for her people believed that Ike had been killed. Other farmers heard the woman's voice and fled. But some of the men summoned courage and waited to observe what was amiss. In their hiding places, they heard Ike's voice calling the fleeing farmers to come back. "Don't run. It's Ike, your son. I'm not a ghost. I'm a living person. Come back mothers."

Hearing his voice, the farmers cautiously tiptoed out of the forest and recognized Ike. But they were still skeptical, not knowing whether he was a living person or a spirit, for they knew that Ike was dead long ago. When they saw two more persons with him, they came out of the bush. Ike recognized a good number of the farmers. He called their names, and rallied them round including the woman that ran first. The woman's heart was still beating fast. She thought she had seen a dead person.

Ike reassured them that he was a living person. Briefly, he narrated his adventure to them. The farmers were overjoyed. They embraced and congratulated him. They were delighted at his escape from Nzom. Seeing that the escapees were tired and hungry, the woman who ran first quickly made a fire and warmed her food and gave the victors.

Some young men had already ran home to inform the people that Ikechukwu Anierobi was alive and was coming home. Like wild fire, the news spread throughout the town. Like bees, Ifite was stirred from their houses. Everybody abandoned their work and took to the road. The village was rocked with shouts of joy and jubilation. Some people rushed to Adaego's house to break the news. When the report reached the local Chief, he was thrilled. He ordered the *Ikolo* gong to be stricken.

Ikolo was a medium device (a large hollowed wooden instrument) through which the natives of Ifite were alerted, invited, or informed of a great happening in the community, whether it was a tragedy, or a glorious incident. When stricken, the sound of *Ikolo* touched the fartherest end of the town, and the natives would begin to head to the Chief's residence to ascertain what was amiss.

With great joy, the Chief ordered a big feast. He requested every traditional music and dancing troupes to converge in his house and to begin a procession to *Ugwu-Omumu-Onwu* to welcome and escort Ike home. He instructed his men to slaughter cows, goats, and cattle for the feast. The whole town was vibrating with joy about Ike's home-coming.

Ifite natives, young and old, were all out of their homes to welcome Ikechukwu Anierobi. In the procession, the Chief and his cabinet were led by his music troupes followed by several traditional dancing groups and drummers. The crowd trudged along the road in great number chanting praises to their heroic son.

When the procession met Ike and his companions on the way, there was a tumultuous acclamation. The drums went higher and higher. The air was rocked with shouting of joy and elation. People were filled with euphoria and jubilation. The Chief embraced Ike and gave him a staff of the highest honour. He also crowned him and let him wear the chieftaincy regalia. The young men carried Ike shoulder high till they arrived in the Chief's compound amidst dancing and merrymaking. They also honoured Oliaku for the part she played in saving their son. She was crowned *Iyom*, a very distinguished women title.

The celebration came to a peak when Ike and Oliaku were escorted round the village square by the Chief and his chieftaincy music troupe, followed by the various traditional dancing groups and music makers. People were thrilled at the colourful event.

It was a memorable occasion which Ifite people would never forget. The village was bustling with joy and merriment. Earlier, the Chief had given instruction that Ike's family be brought to his house to join the celebration. Words could not describe Adaego's joy when she met her missing son. She couldn't believe that Ike was alive. The celebration continued throughout the day. Food and drinks were in abundance.

CHAPTER 26

At Nzom, the King's palace was thrown into confusion and mourning. What happened last night was so horrendous that the King was confounded. He couldn't believe what he saw at the scene of the battle - blood and corpses of his security men. He summoned his cabinet immediately.

His planned ritual ceremony had been torpedoed. It was outrageously incredible. In the history of Nzom, people had never heard of such a calamity. One of the elders described the tragedy as the most humiliating blow ever suffered by a people. The King and his household could not eat. In a feat of rage, he executed many guards.

"It looks like the hands of the gods are in this," one elder remarked.

The incident was a blow to the King, his cabinet, and the Nzom people in general. Everyone was wondering how three securely bounded prisoners could break loose and overpower a bunch of armed guards.

"We must sort this out with the help of the seers," said a red-cap Chief.

"Yes, the soothsayers will tell us what is amiss," said a traditional ruler.

When the cabinet went into session, the King's Court was filled to capacity. The red-cap Chiefs, the clan heads, traditional rulers, elders, and leaders of the people, were all assembled. King Uyanne looked grim and drained. Needless to say, he was ashamed and disappointed about the grisly incident that took place last night. He was engrossed in consternation, so were members of his cabinet.

In this meeting, the King did not appear in his royal diadem. He looked disheveled in his semi-kinship robe. People could tell his frustration, for lines of deep concern furrowed his brow. He started by recounting what took place in his palace the previous night.

"I greet you all," the King began. "I'm sure every one of you had heard what happened last night. Nothing has perplexed me as this."

His eyes were red, a sign that he was fuming.

"In my entire life, nothing has baffled me as this incident. Nothing! Our fathers never witnessed a thing like this. It's unbelievable. *Ears will turn deaf to hear this story, and eyes will go blind.*"

He adjusted his clothes and surveyed the audience. They were all eager to hear what his reaction would be because they knew he was a high-handed monarch. King Uyanne wasn't a stammerer, but today, as he tried to voice his feelings amidst temper, he stammered. The courtroom vibrated with the pique of his frustration.

"I have summoned you so we can discuss what happened last night. We have to figure out how such a thing could happen under our nose. It's hard to believe that my security men and guards were here when it all took place. Why couldn't they challenge three chained prisoners? The hostages might as well have killed the King if they wanted. Are we all women? I must find out the source of this tragedy, and the people behind it must be dealt with. There is no doubt that this is a vicious plot to usurp my throne."

The elders looked at one another at that last remark. King Uyanne seemed to infer that some members of his cabinet and some red cap chiefs who did not like him, and who had eyes on his throne, had connived with his security men to oust him and usurp his monarchy. He felt there was a rebellion here.

The King's short speech engendered a state of apprehension in the audience. Many leaders seemed to agree with the King that there was a plot to dethrone him. Others were simply confused. Nobody spoke after King Uyanne. There was uneasy calm in the courtroom. In a normal court session, the courtroom buzzed with voices of side-talks, sometimes the exchange was rowdy. But today, it was quiet as if nobody was in the chamber. People were stupefied over the tragic incident that took place at night.

After a spell of lull, the cabinet member who spoke was a seasoned elder statesman, Mazi Amuzie Njoku. In his mid-sixties, except for his wrinkled and craggy face, Mazi Njoku looked very strong and healthy. He wasn't only a sagacious clan head, he was by nature, a discerning and astute traditional ruler. Mazi Njoku often frowned at the King's arbitrary decisions. His stance on issues did not always please the King. Although King Uyanne recognized his wisdom and intellectual prowess, he never got on well with Mazy Njoku and men of his type.

This time, people were waiting to hear what Mazi Njoku would say about the awful incident. When he rose on his feet, the courtroom was calm. It was also calm outside. The palace which, a few hours ago, was buzzing and vibrating with joyful celebration, had suddenly assumed a doldrums state. No music was heard. The dancing troupes, the guests, and visitors, had disappeared before dawn. The ceremony had come to an abrupt end following the bloodbath. The King's compound was empty.

Inside the courtroom, consternation and anxiety were almost palpable.

"King Uyanne, my cap is in my hand," Mazi Njoku began. "Chief Abasili I greet you. Chief Ezenwuba, I greet you. Mazi Aniako, I greet you, Chief Ezenwajiaku, I greet you. Chief Ibezim I greet you. My people, I greet you all. The magnitude of the calamity that befell Umuiwu Nzom last night was unspeakable. I have never seen nor heard anything like that. It is undeniably shameful. No one can believe it, but it's real."

He paused and adjusted his chieftaincy robe. For a few moments he appeared lost for words, but he wasn't. That was his style.

"It's amazing that while we were here feasting and preparing for the funeral ceremony of late King Udedibia, such a treacherous incident took place, right under our nose. As King Uyanne said earlier, if the fugitives had wanted, they could've slaughtered the King himself and the rest of us.

"The question I want to ask is: where were the guards when all these things were taking place? How could this have happened when the prison guards were present? We must fathom this mystery. In all the tribal wars we have fought, we have never suffered such a tragic humiliation. Never!"

The audience watched as he gathered momentum.

"Another pertinent question is: who released the prisoners? The three sacrificial men were tied to the stakes. The tethers were so strong and secure that it would be impossible for the men to unfasten the bands without help. Who cut the bands? We saw pieces of rope lying about. Who did it?

"Again, two of the guards who kept watch at the cells are still asleep as we are talking, probably they were drugged. Who drugged them? Presumably, drugging the guards was a strategy to set the prisoners free. Who did all this? These are some of the pertinent questions that require answers, and we need to excavate the answers.

"We know that, apart from the guards, the only person in the King's palace that has access to the barn was the King's daughter, Oliaku. We know that Oliaku was the only person authorized to feed the captives. She also served the guards their meal. Who else could have poisoned their food? Again, the young girl was said to have ran away with the prisoners. I venture to say that the King's daughter, not only knew something about the prisoners' escape, but also was an accomplice and actually played a significant role in this ugly business. I dare say that *what ails the withering otulu (*a plant*), is lodging beneath otulu's root.*"

The people looked at themselves, and then looked at the King. Quiet murmur ran through the hall like a wave. Mazi Amuzie Njoku was alluding that the mystery of the horrendous act was traceable to the rank and file of the cabinet members and ostensibly abated by the King's own daughter. Therefore, if the King was looking for the perpetrators of this appalling incident, he should start with his men and his daughter.

The audience was amazed at Njoku's courageous outburst. He did not mince words. His speech *ruffled the King's feathers* and those of his closest friends. They whispered privately and exchanged insinuations, but no one had the nerves to say that the King's daughter was actively involved in what took place in the palace last night.

Mazi Amuzie Njoku was one of the few fearless men in the council who had the courage to *call a spade a spade, rather than an excavating instrument.* He was vocal, and often stood by the truth without minding *whose ox was being gored.*

People were moved by his speech. They had also heard that during the scuffle, the King's daughter was yelling to one prisoner: "Run, run, run, save your life! Run, run, run, they are coming!"

"Abomination!" said one elder, snapping his finger. "Incredible!"

Although the meeting was calm, tension was almost tangible. People were glued to their seats. Nobody moved nor adjusted in his chair. Shame and humiliation appeared on the King's face at the mention of his daughter and her involvement.

Next, Chief Abor, one of the intellectual giants, gave a short speech.

"While I agree that the seers and soothsayers in this land should be brought here to dig out the mystery surrounding this incident, I want to state that we must take a critical look at our custom of burying the dead with the living. The tradition is outdated and must be disconti…"

"No! No! No!" the crowd interrupted. They looked at one another as if Chief Abor had spoken a blasphemy and must be stoned or at least banished. He disregarded their opposition and proceeded to criticize the obsolete culture.

"I had made this representation before in one of our gatherings, but nobody seemed to recognize how disagreeable the practice was. I don't see any sense in burying a dead person with human head. It's meaningless. Though it's our culture and was practiced by our ancestors years ago, it's obnoxious and purposeless. The time has come for us to do away with this antiquated way of life.

"Many towns and villages have dropped the practice years ago," he went on. "I think it was wisdom, not ignorance, that made those towns abandon ritual burial. I don't support the continuation of this human sacrifice. It is an outmoded tradition. Thank you."

He sat down.

The crowd buzzed with approval and disapproval of Chief Abor's speech. Some people agreed with him, some did not. Some members of the cabinet looked at him with suspicion.

The two men that had spoken sparked dissension in people's minds. The atmosphere in the courtroom was tense. The chiefs were particularly worried that Mazi Njoku indicted the King's daughter in his speech.

CHAPTER 27

An uneasy calm still reigned. Nobody spoke after Chief Abor. Then came thunder from a radical rightist, Chief Udemezue Onyije. He was a stunted man with patterned tribal marks. He was another influential member of the King's royalties. He looked sad. He grated his teeth and began,

"King Uyanne, I greet you. The man who had just spoken does not deserve to be a member of the King's cabinet. Why on earth should he condemn the peoples' culture - the age-long tradition of our fathers? Who can hear this? I hope the ancestors did not hear this blasphemy, otherwise they will ...," he swallowed.

He ranted and raved as he poured out his anger vociferously. His opinion was conservative and his words were satirically harsh. He was protective of the ritual killing. People watched the dramatic behaviour that laced his address.

Chief Onyije's argument registered a positive impression on his fellow chiefs. He succeeded in pulling many people to his side. Some chiefs agreed with him about the preservation of the culture. But many had their reservations.

"This man they call Abor must be banished," Chief Onyije spewed, disrespectfully. "He is not worthy to be one of us. His loyalty is questionable. He must be watched. The ritual has been with us for generations, and Abor is telling us to scrap it. How can a King be buried like an ordinary man? I suggest Abor should be stripped of his titles and investigated."

Chief Udemezue Onyije was still speaking when another radical, Udo Udoma, stopped him. A 69 year-old hunter with a dropping shoulder, Chief Udoma had rhetoric ability and delivered astonishing judgment to his subjects with incredible traditional jurisprudence. Today everybody was eager to hear him.

"We have heard enough of that offensive rhetoric," said Chief Udoma. "We must learn to respect fellow red cap Chiefs irrespective of the opinion they advance. Everybody is entitled to his opinion, we may get angry, but we should not run riot with rage. Chief Onyije, you used excessive harsh words to address Chief Abor, a fellow cabinet member, as though he was an ordinary man.

"We are here today because the men we captured for the burial of our late King escaped. Only God knows how. They not only escaped from bondage, they slaughtered many of the King's bodyguards. Isn't that a shame? But that's not where I am going. What I want to say is simple. After this meeting, we must still bury the King whose body has been lying in state for over a month. We will either bury him without human heads, or look for more heads. The pertinent question here is: why should we look for heads when we have surplus heads amongst us?"

He paused and watched the people's reaction. The men appeared confused. They seemed not to understand what he was talking about.

"*We have drums, why should we drum on our stomachs?*" Chief Udoma went on. "Everybody sitting in this room has a head, why don't we cut our own heads for the ritual? The simple thing to do is to chop off a couple of heads amongst us and the business is done. We could get more if we so desire."

The red cap chiefs looked at one another in amazement. "Has he been drinking today?" one chief whispered to another beside him.

"I'm not sure he had had any drink this morning," replied the chief, "but let's listen to what he is saying. It appears he is making some sense."

"I suggest we use our own heads to bury the late King instead of hunting for the heads of other people," Chief Udoma continued. "Who would volunteer a head? We have more than enough. Those who would like to volunteer their heads or the heads of their sons for the funeral, raise your hands."

He looked around. No hands went up. Instead, the chiefs and the elders looked at him puzzled. They kept whispering among themselves. While some people made no sense out of what he said, others considered his speech logically sagacious.

"My people," Chief Udoma went on, "our adage says: *The chicken's eggs are wealth, but that of the guinea fowl are meat.* Nothing is as sweet as life. All of us love and cherish our lives and we cling to it tenaciously. Similarly, other people cherish their lives and cling to it. Nobody wants to die. Life is sweet as long as it lasts. That's why those captives broke loose and escaped. They cherish their existence.

"Having said this, I want us to take a second look at this tradition. It is true that this custom has been with us for generations; it is true that our fathers practiced it and handed it down to us; it is also true that our ancestors held the ritual in a very high esteem; but I must say that things have changed. Today is not yesterday. Our forefathers did these things out of ignorance. They thought they were doing service to the dead. But today, we know better. We should know that this ritual is meaningless. We should know it is waste of lives. We must know that it is inappropriate to kill an innocent man for no reason other than that we want to bury the dead King with the man's head. It's absurd! I suggest we do away with this custom."

Chief Udoma's erudite speech went into many hearts and stirred controversy. While some elders saw his speech as irresponsible, many saw it as noteworthy. His argument moved minds and made many Chiefs question the rationale in the age-long custom.

Many chiefs were convinced that the human sacrifice was absolutely unnecessary and should be discontinued. The traditional rulers, who were about to send emissaries for another head-hunt, seemed to see things differently after listening to Chief Udoma.

Before he took his seat, Chief Udoma said more things critical of the ritual sacrifice. After that, many people became convinced that the observance of this custom was old-fashioned and should be dropped.

Another man, Chief Oranyelugo, a close associate of King Uyanne, spoke and condemned the obnoxious tradition. His stance on the issue was a surprise, for people thought that he would pitch camp with the King no matter what. But he spoke his mind.

Chief Oranyelugo urged the Nzom leaders and elders to drop the culture and watch how the gods react to it. Describing the ritual as the ignorant performance of the ancestors, he said: "If we must retain this culture, we must be prepared to bury our kings with the heads of our sons. Furthermore, anybody going out to hunt for human heads, must be prepared to face the wrath of the White men who are trying to wipe out outrageous customs and traditions like this one. I can't say more than this."

He sat down.

King Uyanne looked frozen. His right-hand man, who used to stand firmly behind him on all issues, had abandoned him in this case. It was apparent that the majority of the cabinet would decamp, if there was a vote, because Chief Oranyelugo was not with the King. His words were weighty and highly respected and often taken seriously. The King sensed that if he did not accept the opinions of these respected cabinet members, his throne was in danger.

Many chiefs spoke after Chief Oranyelugo, some of them spoke in favour of preserving the ritual, but majority of the chiefs spoke against it. The popular opinion was to scrap the ritual practice and to bury Kings like everyone else.

King Uyanne was in a dilemma. In the end, he said,

"From the opinion expressed in this gathering, it's apparent that many people do not want the performance of this age-long tradition to continue. However, we cannot, here and now, decide to drop it. It's a far-reaching issue that requires serious deliberation. I therefore, urge you to go home and sleep over it.

"In the meantime, the burial ceremony of my father should go ahead as planned. We must accomplish the funeral, albeit, without a human head. When we finish the funeral, we then decide what to do next. If we decide to continue the tradition, we will exhume the body and complete the funeral, if not, so be it."

CHAPTER 28

At Ifite, things were going well with the Anierobi family since Ike's return from Nzom. Life continued as usual.

Today Emeka had gone to the market to sell some vegetables he harvested from the farm. When he came back, Adaego looked at him in disbelief. Clearly, she wasn't happy.

"You're back already?" she asked Emeka. Her face looked glum.

"Sure," Emeka replied gleefully. He rested his basket at a corner and slumped into a chair. He was tired.

"It doesn't take you time to sell these things," Adaego said quizzically, "do you give the food items away?"

Emeka sensed dissatisfaction in his mother's words. "Nne allow me to rest, I'm tired. You don't expect me to sit among the market women to sell my stuff piecemeal, do you?"

"What's wrong with that?" Adaego challenged. "How do you sell your goods?"

"Why these questions? Can I have some rest?" Emeka said, his face contoured.

"I'm just curious. I want to know how you carry out your transactions with customers. Don't you bargain?"

"The important thing is that I have sold the commodities."

"No! Perhaps the important thing, my son, is how much money you made, and to what extent your efforts in the farm were rewarded. Not how fast you sold the items. Can you explain to me how you sell these things?"

"I hand them over to the women retailers."

"There you are. At any price convenient for them?"

"Not so. At a price convenient for me. I bargain."

"Your bargaining is as good as giving the things away," Adaego remarked and hissed.

Emeka scratched his head in protest. He kicked a bucket sitting in front of him to demonstrate his displeasure. Adaego ignored that act.

Emeka was irritated by his mother's disturbing inquiries regarding how he sold the items he took to the market every day. He didn't like to sit among the market women to sell his foodstuff in small bits in order to make more money. But that was what his mother preferred. Emeka hated to do so.

Adaego would not argue any more. The bottom line was that she wasn't satisfied with the way Emeka sold the things he took to the market. She believed the boy was cheated. She thought he never made enough money in his sales. He simply gave away his foodstuff. There was nothing she could do. She couldn't go to the market herself. She left everything as it were. After all, Emeka was a child playing the role of an adult. Therefore, no matter how he tried to be perfect, there must be flaws and lapses here and there.

After that little clash Emeka left the room and hurried to the kitchen to find his breakfast. Ike was in the kitchen already eating.

"Ike, who did you know in Lagos?" Emeka asked as he stepped into the kitchen.

"Excuse me?" Ike replied.

"Do you know anybody in Lagos?"

"What do you mean?"

"You got a letter from Lagos, I met Chike Olisa on the way and he gave me a letter for you. He said one of the apprentice boys at Onitsha gave him the letter to give you."

Ike was a little confused. He did not know anybody in Lagos, neither did he remember writing anybody at Lagos. All the same he took the envelope with curiosity and tore it. He read the title:

APPOINTMENT FOR AN INTERVIEW

"Aah! aah! aah! this is it!" Ike shouted blissfully. This is it, this is it!"

"What's that?" Emeka asked curiously, a plate in one hand and a stool on the other. "What's the jubilation about?"

"This is the reply of an application for a job I wrote to Lagos long ago. I have forgotten all about it, and now they wrote inviting me for an interview. Oh, I'm so happy. I need this. I hope it works."

"Would you go to Lagos if it worked?" Emeka asked with reservation.

"Why not?"

Emeka did not like the idea. Lagos was far. It's like going to another country. He asked again,

"What are you going to Lagos to do? You have never been to Lagos. Do you know anybody in Lagos?"

Ike did not answer those questions. He was happy to receive a reply to his application, and if he was lucky to get a job in Lagos, he would be more than happy to work at the capital city of the Federal Republic of Nigeria. That's very important to him.

The letter came from The Peoples Bank of Nigeria, Lagos. The bank was recruiting workers for an expansion project.

Ike had sent out several applications to different places when he was at Onitsha. He had forgotten everything about those applications, but today, he received a reply to one of them. His heart was filled with joy, and he did not listen to his brother's misgivings about going to Lagos where crime was said to be the order of the day.

Home folks heard a lot of bad stories about Lagos. Anybody going to Lagos in those days was warned to be careful.

Adaego was in her room listening. She heard her children's conversation about a job and trip to Lagos. She swore in her heart, even before Ike came to her with the news, that she was not going to allow it. Adaego was the authority in the house. What she said must apply.

He wants to go there and die, she said to herself as she eavesdropped at the conversation between her two sons. I will not allow that to happen. This boy wants to die before his time. Three months ago he survived human sacrifice at the hands of Nzom people. Now he wants to undertake another dangerous adventure to a foreign land. Not in my house. I won't allow this to happen. There may not be another Oliaku in Lagos to save him. He is not going anywhere.

Although Ike did not know where Lagos was nor how to get there, he was anxious to attend the interview because he needed a job. Since he came back from Nzom, he had been idling about, doing nothing, and feeling boredom. He didn't know how to begin life anew. He was getting worried and frustrated about his situation - what to do with his life after all the tribulations. He had already had a checkered history at his young age.

Oliaku had just returned from the river and met the raging discussion. She put down her water pot and listened. She couldn't make any sense of the argument between Ike and Emeka. Ike's appointment at Lagos had ignited a burning question in the house. She heard them saying:

"You're not going to Lagos."

"Yes, I'm going."

"No, Lagos is dangerous."

"I have to go. I'll be all right."

Oliaku watched the scene for a few minutes and left them alone. She was hungry too.

"Has everybody eaten their breakfast?" she asked holding a wooden spoon on one hand and a plate on the other.

"Yes," Adaego responded from her room, "it's all yours my daughter. Take all that is left."

Oliaku hurried back to the kitchen happily to attack the remaining *ukwa* (breadfruit) meal. She loved *ukwa* so much and always asked for the menu. She carried the earthen pot of *ukwa* and joined the others in their mother's room where they were still debating the Lagos trip.

"What's going on?" she asked between mouthfuls.

Emeka quickly told her that Ike was planning to leave them. He presented a grotesque analysis of the matter to instigate Oliaku to discourage Ike from his plans. Oliaku wore a dismal look after hearing about a trip to Lagos. In the first place, she wasn't happy about Ike leaving the house, but she needed more information. She seemed to be more protective of Ike than anyone else.

"Where is Lagos?" she asked naively.

"Lagos is very far away in the Western part of Nigeria," Emeka attempted a geographical explanation. Oliaku did not understand. She did not go to school.

"Where is that?" She asked.

"Don't listen to him," Ike interrupted. "Lagos is not far, but it is a big city in Nigeria."

"Where is Nigeria?"

"Huh!" Emeka snorted, already getting bored of the geography tutorial.

Oliaku was trying to understand where Lagos was to determine whether to support the trip or not. In any case, whether it was far or near, she didn't want Ike to leave home.

Ike had made up his mind to go to Lagos, and nothing would stop him. He had an iron-clad will that would shame the tiger. Anything he set his mind to accomplish, nothing would deter him. Emeka was the only person who understood that this was an integral part of his brother's personality.

Oliaku began to coax Ike to forget Lagos, but he would not. She was not happy. She became depressed even before the trip. Whenever she remembered that Ike would soon leave them, she hid herself at a corner and cried quietly. She knew she was going to miss him. She had become attached to Ike whom she looked upon as her elder brother.

Ike loved Oliaku so much. Often he wondered in what way he was going to compensate the young lady for saving his life from the hands of Nzom people. Every member of the family gave Oliaku preferential treatment. Everybody pampered her, even Emeka who was about the same age. They were forever indebted to her for saving Ike's life. The bond that held the family together was strong. They had all formed a phalanx in the Anierobi family.

Since her flight from Nzom, Oliaku had been living with the Anierobi family.

She had become part of Adaego's household. Adaego received her with open heart. She was more than grateful to the young girl for saving her son's life. Adaego was amazed at Oliaku's heroism, a feat she said only a few men could accomplish. Without question, she had adopted Oliaku and treated her as her own child and as a member of her family, so did her children.

CHAPTER 29

The following day, the issue of Lagos came up again. Ike pleaded with Oliaku and the rest of the family to allow him to pursue his life objective. "I have to find something to do," he explained to Oliaku who kept following him everywhere begging him not to go to Lagos. "I'm rotting away here. I need to find work. Besides, I'm not leaving forever. I will be visiting home."

"But that place is very far," Oliaku whined. "We won't see you any more."

"Not so. I'll visit home often, trust me," he said, touching her lips lovingly with a finger.

"Are you sure?" Oliaku asked.

"I'm positive, and besides, I have not passed the interview.

"Which one is *itavuu*?" Oliaku asked oafishly.

"An interview is the art of asking questions as a test of knowledge. Potential employees are interviewed to select the best candidates for a job," Ike elaborated. "By the way, the fact that I was invited for an interview does not necessarily mean that I've been offered the job. I may not be selected. I may fail the interview."

"That's true anyway." Emeka admitted.

"I know you'll pass the *itavuu*," Oliaku said assuredly, "You are intelligent."

"That's a good point," Emeka agreed as he examined a small wound on his leg. He pressed a finger on the sore gingerly and grimaced. "He is very bright, I know it. I can't see Ike failing any exam. He has already passed the interview. He is only going there to pick up the job."

Despite everybody's opposition, Ike was determined to make the best of this opportunity. This might be the beginning of a new chapter in my life, he thought, after reading the letter. I may be one of the lucky applicants, who knows?

He read the piece of paper over and over to make sure he didn't miss anything.

He knelt down and thanked God, asking Him to help make it a success. Emeka and Adaego were watching the drama. Emeka smiled cynically. His main concern was Ike's safety. He was worried because Lagos was very far and was a crime infested area.

Emeka knew that the capital city was sophisticated. He had read many things in his Geography and Social Studies about Lagos. He also knew they had no relations in Lagos where his brother would stay. He did not want anything to happen to Ike again.

There was something Ike had not thought about – transportation. Lagos transport fare was very high and he had no money. He had no source of income. The little money Emeka realized from the sale of vegetables and fruits, was used to feed the family. Things were getting rougher and tougher for the family, and this trip to Lagos required fund.

Ike wished that the interview was at Onitsha where transportation cost would be manageable. Nevertheless, he was delighted to be invited to Lagos.

Only three days was left for the interview deadline. He must decide what to do, and quickly too. The postmark on the envelope was September 2nd. He received it on Tuesday, October 1st. The interview was scheduled for October 4th. The letter had been lying at Onitsha.

Initially, everybody had objected to the Lagos trip, now everybody, not only gave way, but also offered financial support for the trip.

It was certain now that Ike was ready to leave. His mother gave him two pounds, but he refused. That was the only money the woman had. When Ike declined to accept the money, Adaego began to cry: "Please take it my son, I don't want you to suffer at Lagos."

"No, you have no money," Ike told her. "Keep it in case you have an emergency. Don't worry about me. I'll take care of myself."

"I insist you take the money, you might..."

"No mother, I'll find my way to Lagos."

Oliaku gave Ike two shillings and two pence. That was all the money she had too. She also offered Ike her necklace to sell and raise some money. But Ike refused to take anything from her.

The following morning, which was Wednesday, October 2nd, Ike left for Onitsha on his first leg to Lagos. Everybody, especially Oliaku, was crying. It was like a funeral scene. But Ike was determined to pursue his career. With the little money Emeka scratched out from the feeding purse, Ike took a courageous stride into the unknown world, yet for another adventure. He wasn't afraid of the unknown. In order to conquer the unknown, the unknown must be challenged.

CHAPTER 30

First, Ike stopped at Onitsha to see the apprentice boys. He avoided No 3 Ekwulobia Street where he lived with his uncle Ufele. He never wanted to see that building again in his life. He prayed he'd not bump into Ufele. He didn't want to see him or any member of his household. He had sworn he'd never set foot at Onitsha, but necessity had compelled him to *stoop and lick his sputum*.

Today he was at Onitsha. He stopped first at Ejiofor's store. Ejiofor was one of Ufele's apprentices. He was still serving. He and Ike were good chums when Ike was in Ufele's service.

Ejiofor jumped up with joy at seeing Ike. He almost pushed him down when he leapt onto him. They hugged and shook hands. They were delighted to see each other. They talked. Ejiofor narrated many things that had taken place since Ike left Onitsha. He had many more stories to tell but Ike stopped him:

"Listen Ejiofor, I have to cut you short. I'm in a hurry. Besides, I don't want Ufele to see…"

"Why?" Ejiofor interrupted admiring his tall structure. Ike had grown so tall within these few years. "I thought you have come back to stay with us?"

"Come back?" Ike repeated and laughed. "Come back here? Are you crazy?"

"I heard that our master was begging you to return to business. You know he regretted dismissing you. Nobody wanted you to leave. People here love you so much. Why can't you come back?"

"Ejiofor leave that matter. I don't want to go into it. I am on my way to Lagos."

"Wait a minute, Lagos? Lagos, to do what? What's wrong with staying here?"

"Never!" Ike declared.

"You have a good prospect here you know."

"To hell with Ufele's business."

Ejiofor stared at him disappointed. He thought Ike had come back to join them.

Ike rested his bag at a corner and sat at the edge of Ejiofor's desk. He was sweating. It was a long walk from the motor-park. Ejiofor observed that Ike had lost weight. Although he was taller now, he looked slim. Poor boy, Ejiofor thought, he has gone through a lot of hard times. He must be starving in the village.

"What's your plan then?" Ejiofor asked with disappointment.

"That's why I came to see you, and I don't want Ufele nor any member of his family to know that I came here."

"Oh, don't worry about that. Our master is not home. He went to Aba yesterday."

"O yea?"

"Yes. And he will not return until Saturday evening. What are you going to Lagos to do?"

"In search of job," Ike replied and felt more relaxed now that he learnt that Ufele was not home. "I have appointment for an interview."

"Interview, for what?"

"For employment. I told you I'm searching for a job."

Ejiofor cast a sympathetic look at him. It seemed to him that Ike was really suffering because he said he was looking for a job. It pained him that Ike had to go through a lot of distress. He recalled in his heart the tragedy at Nzom where Ike nearly lost his life. He did not want to discuss that. He wished that Ike could stay with them at Onitsha, and in a few years, or even months, Ufele would *settle* him and he'd start his own business. He believed Ike would do very well in business life. He tried to persuade him to stay, but Ike had made up his mind.

"But why Lagos? Why not look for work at Onitsha?" Ejiofor asked.

"I tried but I couldn't get one. I applied to several places when I was with you. Just yesterday, I got a letter from Lagos, and I have to go immediately before the interview date expires. If they accept me, I'll be glad to work in Lagos. If not, I'll come back home."

Ejiofor studied Ike compassionately. "Ike, I admire your courage," he said almost in tears. "You are a brave and determined individual. Your mettle is admirable. Sometimes I wish I had a fraction of the grit you possess. If I were academically endowed as you, Oh, I would love it. But I'm not brilliant. My brain is hardened, like this iron pillar. It's amazing how you were able to read at home and obtain the School Certificate equivalent. You're amazing! I wish I had half the gift of intelligence you have."

"I believe you have even more," Ike said modestly. "I'm not smarter than you are. All of us have potentials. All we need is to develop and utilize them. I really don't think I have more intelligence than you or anybody else."

Ejiofor recalled Ike's humility and hardwork. "When you were carrying books and papers about, no one knew what you were gunning for. We did not know you were working towards a goal until we heard you had passed your GCE papers. You are incredible! We admire you, all of us. You are amazing! Despite what happened last year, everybody in the yard still admires you. People love and cherish you."

Ejiofor was referring to the love affair between Ike and Angela which culminated into Ike's expulsion from Ufele's company. Neither Ejiofor nor Ike wanted to go into that incident. It was left out of their conversation.

"They speak well of you. I'm yet to see anybody in the yard that does not cherish your charisma. When the news of your return from Nzom reached Onitsha, it was a great event. Everybody was jubilating. In fact, the apprentice boys celebrated it in a special way."

Ike was delighted to hear all these good stories and testimonies. He was glad that people at Onitsha still respected him, despite what happened. He was happy they had forgiven the mistake he made and that they still feel good about him.

On a serious note, Ike explained his plans to Ejiofor. He also made his financial problem known to him. "One of the problems I'm facing at home is poverty," Ike said as he ate the lunch Ejiofor bought for him. "I have no money at all, but I am determined to travel to Lagos for this interview. I can't afford to miss it. That's the only chance I have to get a job.

Ejiofor was Ike's best friend when he was at Onitsha. They were closer than any other member of Ufele's apprentice squad. After his story, Ejiofor was apt to respond to his request for help. He offered Ike an amazing sum of two pounds. Ike was stunned. Although he knew that Ejiofor would help him, he didn't expect that much. Ejiofor also volunteered to talk to other apprentice boys on Ike's behalf.

When Ike finished with Ejiofor, he went from one store to another greeting his old friends and former co-apprentice boys. They were so happy to see him. Some of them were so enchanted that they jumped on him ecstatically. They thought Ike was back to rejoin them. But briefly he explained his mission. They urged him to stay at least overnight. Ike was reluctant to do so.

Wherever he went, the story was the same. They wanted him to spend the night with them. They mounted pressure on him. They knew his fears, and they told him that Ufele was not home.

Ike was ambivalent about their request to stay overnight. He did not want to be seen at No 3 Ekwulobia Street Onitsha. He hated to bump into someone he wouldn't like to see, for example, Angela's parents, or anybody in that household. But for his financial problem, nothing would've brought him to Onitsha in the first place. Nothing would've brought him to that damned yard where he believed he smeared his name with cow dung. Nevertheless, he liked to be with his old friends, the apprentice boys.

He had already started cracking jokes with them reminiscent of their companionship when he was in Ufele's service. The jokes reminded them of those good old days. They all laughed and talked nostalgically. All the boys were united in their opinion that Ike should spend the night with them.

"If you don't spend the night with us, I will die," Mr. K said. He appeared more excited than anyone else to meet Ike. "You must spend the night with us, or else I will drop dead."

Everybody laughed. Eventually Ike caved in.

It was twilight, the purple stain of night was deepening slowly when Ufele's boys smuggled Ike into Number 3 Ekwulobia Street Onitsha, without a soul knowing. They feasted and talked throughout the night enjoying his company.

The following day, very early in the morning, Ike took off for Lagos. His friends had collected a total of ten pounds among themselves to facilitate his trip to Lagos. That was quite a big sum. It was more than enough for Ike to meet his transportation and lodging expenses. He was so happy for their support. In a brief ceremony that marked his departure to Lagos, Ike expressed his appreciation to his friends in the following words:

"I cannot find words to express my feelings and gratitude to you for your love and kindness. I sincerely appreciate your support. I didn't expect this much. You surprised me a great deal. Thank you so much. I still

remember our lovely days, how we used to stay together and crack jokes. The sweet memory of our company is still fresh in my mind. I have not forgotten it. I wish I could spend more time with you, but I have to go. One day, we shall all meet and sit together to celebrate and to tell the stories of our lives – the apprentice boys. I love you all."

CHAPTER 31

Big trucks that carried goods and merchandise from Onitsha to Lagos were virtually the only mode of public transportation at that time. And there was no bridge from Onitsha to Asaba. The Niger Bridge was built several years before the Nigerian civil war. Prior to that time, you must cross the River Niger to Asaba by boat on your way to Lagos. Large barges and giant steamer-boats ferried motor vehicles across the Niger.

Ike boarded one of the lorries bound to Lagos. He had never seen a giant boat or a big engine craft. For him, it was a new experience and he was delighted. While the passengers in the steamer were falling asleep, Ike was looking around enjoying the trip. He saw fishermen in the River Niger, far off. This brought some sad memory to him. He recalled his ordeal at the Nzom fishing pond. That grim experience will always live with him. As they approached the shore on the other side of the Niger, he saw children swimming at the bank. He saw market women coming down to the shore with their loads to cross the river to Onitsha.

After crossing the bridge, Ike's journey to Lagos began in earnest. His vehicle left Asaba at 2:30 p.m. Occasionally he looked through the wooden frames of the vehicle watching trees and shrubs flying past. He had never undertaken such a long journey. When some passengers began to eat their snacks, which would pass for dinner, Ike brought out a wrap of roasted groundnuts and a small bunch of banana and began to eat. The lorry traveled the whole night and reached Lagos the following morning which was Friday the 4th of October, the interview date.

Ike had earlier made inquiries and obtained directions from some traders in the vehicle who had knowledge of Lagos. Without wasting time, he boarded the *bolikeja* mini-bus and headed to the location of the interview. When he got at the venue, applicants were already queuing up. The long line of attendants snaked off into the street.

Ike arrived right on time. He was very happy. There were many applicants. Ike was worried about the large number of candidates. He thought this might narrow down his chances. But he prayed that his luck would shine.

Peoples Bank is one of the leading financial institutions in Nigeria. Part of its current expansion project was the establishment of new branches in many parts of the federation. The recruitment drive was centred on young school leavers who would work in the new branches. Those who did exceptionally well after the initial training, would undergo a four-year degree program in Accountancy.

Eventually, depending on their performance, they would head the new branches.

Ike was nervously excited. His hope lay on the successful outcome of this interview. If he succeeded, he would be glad to work anywhere they posted him, even if it's in hell. If he failed, he would return to Ifite, in the East, to till the soil.

"Oh God, be my help," he prayed as he watched the crowd that came for the interview. "God, I have suffered enough in this life. I hope I'll succeed, help me."

Many candidates from different parts of Nigeria attended the interview. Applicants with West African School Certificate (WASC), General Certificate of Education (GCE), Commercial School graduates, and even First School Leaving Certificate (FSLC) holders, converged at the venue for the selection. The location was The Murani Boys Secondary School (MBSS), Olorunsogo, Lagos.

After eight hours the interview was over. All candidates were interviewed. In his assessment, Ike believed he did well, both in the written assignment and the oral questions, his guts told him. He was optimistic.

Although he felt he did well at the interview, that was only one side of the equation. There was the other side - the problem of favouritism. This would be a big huddle for him because he had no one to speak for him. Many candidates had *links,* and *connections.* How good a candidate performed in the interview was not the only yardstick for choosing a candidate. In Nigerian style, if you did not know someone who knew someone, your chances were very slim.

Before they were let go, candidates were told to report back the following Monday to receive their results. They were also told that from that day, successful candidates would consider themselves employed, and their salaries would begin to count. Ike could not help being euphoric.

Ike had no place to stay until Monday, but he wasn't alone. There were many applicants from far places who had no place to squat until Monday. Good a thing, Ike had some money that could sustain him for one week and more.

When all the candidates had left the MBSS premises, those without a place to go remained in the school compound loitering. As the dusk gathered, these applicants drifted aimlessly around the stores in the streets, buying food and snacks waiting for night-fall.

They stopped passersby and asked questions about cheap hotels. They talked with each other and gradually discovered themselves. They had a common problem - where to stay until Monday. They formed a group and began to plan how to tackle their problem.

The school dormitories were vacated because teachers were on strike.

"Suppose we squat in these empty dorms," suggested one of the candidates dolefully.

"That will be wonderful," replied another student, "but can they allow us? Everywhere is locked."

"Unless we ask, we'll not know," Ike said over the shoulder of the last speaker.

The stranded applicants were desperate for a place to rest their heads until Monday. The prevailing idea was to squat in the students dorms. As they discussed their plight, new ideas emerged. Eventually they decided to go to the Principal's house to obtain permission to sleep in the dormitory until Monday.

A few applicants were delegated to see the Principal. Ike was among them. When they got to the Principal's house, Mr. Olarewaju was not at home. The team decided to see the Vice Principal.

An off-duty gateman volunteered to take them to the Vice Principal's house. Luckily the man was at home. He was just coming back from his evening tennis. A tall figure with a vacant expression, Mr. Amos Mobolaji, had lost a lot of his hair at forty.

After the visitors had explained their predicament, Mr. Mobolaji authorized them to occupy the Chief Johnson Akerele Dormatory at the slope leading to the school kitchen. He asked the gateman to unlock the hall for them.

The strangers were allowed to stay in the dormitory until Monday. Nobody would be allowed to remain in the school property after Monday. The candidates were very happy. They promised to abide by the agreement.

At the crack of dawn on Monday, candidates had lined up to receive the result of the interview. The queue stretched from the front door of the administrative block to the street. Shortly afterwards, the Assistant General Manager of the Peoples Bank, Mr. Ambali Gbadamosi, emerged with two long sheets containing the names of selected candidates.

As he pulled out the two sheets, Ike's heart missed a beat. Other hearts might have missed some beats too. Heads hung listlessly as anxiety gripped everyone. Ike was anxious. Some applicants were perspiring due to tension. People waited expectantly in the queue staring at the man as though he held the key to their lives.

"As in every examination," the Manager began, adjusting his silver-rimmed glasses, "some participants will be successful, while others will not. I'm going to paste these sheets on the billboard. If you see your name on the list, you're successful, if not, try again next time.

"Successful candidates automatically resume duty from today," Mr. Mobolaji continued. "The management of this organization is aware that some of you came from distant places, and you will need time to prepare for the job. In this respect, you are allowed one week off, with pay, to get prepared. You are expected to report to the office next Monday for orientation. Any candidate who failed to show up on Monday should consider him or herself not part of this agency."

The security guards walked around soberly, hands behind their backs, making sure that everything was orderly. The applicants at the back of the line were surging forward. Everybody was struggling to be in front.

No soon had the man pasted the results on the bulletin board than they broke the orderliness. Candidates swarmed around the bulletin board like stirred bees gazing at the sheets on the wall for their names. The security took charge and compelled everybody to file in a single line. Order was restored. Applicants came forward one by one to check their names.

They moved away from the line after seeing their results. Many applicants saw their names and jumped up for joy. Many were not as lucky, they walked away coldly.

Ike was far behind the line, but as the queue tapered off, he approached. He had said all the prayers he knew in his heart. There was nothing he did not promise God. He knew his future depended on this job. If he failed the interview, he might not have another opportunity.

"God have mercy on thy child," he continued to pray as he wiped trickles of sweat from his brow. His lips were dry and parched, and he kept them busy mumbling silent prayers.

While he was meditating with his face down, the man in front of him moved forward in the line leaving a gap. Ike did not know. The man behind him tapped his shoulder. He jerked into live and trudged forward to close the gap.

Soon he was standing behind the applicant who was now searching his name at the billboard. The young man was shaking. He ran down the list with a trembling forefinger. Ike could observe the finger shivering, like one with Parkinson disease, out of anxiety. This man saw his name and threw his hands up in jubilation. Ike muttered a congratulatory note to him.

It was Ike's turn. His heart skipped countless beats. His eyes were running through the list. At the upper left corner of the sheet, he saw his name, IKECHUKWU ANIEROBI. He screamed, "Thank you Lord!"

The same young man he congratulated earlier said to him, "Seen your name?"

"Yes," Ike replied ecstatically. "I made it."

"Congratulations!" the boy told him with handshake.

"Thank you."

They were happy. They watched other applicants briefly as they looked up their results. Some came out rejoicing; others came out cheerless and morose.

Ike and his new friend talked for a while about the interview.

"This is the hardest interview I ever attended," said the young man.

"Definitely," Ike agreed, even though he didn't find the interview challenging.

The two candidates strolled across the field chatting. The man was telling Ike that he had been searching for work for a long time.

"And you have found one," Ike said. "By the way, my name is Ikechukwu Anierobi. You can call me Ike."

"Cool. I'm glad to meet you Ike. My name is Ade Babalola."

"Ade it's a pleasure to meet you."

"Thank you. It's good to bump into a good-natured guy. You're from Eastern Nigeria?"

"Yes."

"I'm from Western Nigeria."

"What part of Western Nigeria?" Ike asked and adjusted his short knickers.

"Oyo Town," Ade replied. "And you"?

"Onitsha Province."

"The busy commercial city. Did you travel all the way from Onitsha for the interview?" Ade asked and stooped to pick up his pen that dropped.

"Yes. It was a long journey."

"I know. I can see you're tired."

"Did you travel from Oyo for the interview or do you live..."

"Oh no," Ade interrupted. "I live here in Lagos with my parents."

"Good for you," Ike said. "You don't need to worry about where to stay until Monday."

"No. What about you? Do you have a relation in Lagos?"

"No. I have nobody here, neither do I know anybody," Ike said in despair. "To start with, I have never been to Lagos."

"Oh, do you plan to start work at once on Monday?" Ade asked tucking his loose shirt.

"Of course, I have to. I don't want to miss this opportunity."

"I agree with you. One has to consolidate what one has."

"Do you know of a cheap hotel where I can lodge until Monday?"

"Would you like to stay with me in my house?" Ade offered.

"In your house?"

"Yes."

"That will be terrific if you don't mind."

"I don't mind."

"Will that be okay with your people?"

"O yes. You can stay with me," Ade assured him confidently.

Ike's face beamed with delight. His problem was solved.

"I'm so happy to have met you Ade," Ike said. "You're so kind."

"My parents will be glad to meet you. They will be willing to accommodate you in our house. We have a big house at Ikeja. My siblings are all grown and gone. I'm the only one staying with the old folks. Many rooms are empty in our house. Let's go."

He picked up one of Ike's bags and led the way.

Things were beginning to fall into shape for Ike. He said the Almighty God was answering his prayers. He had got a permanent job and his friend had offered to squat him for some time.

Ike was well received by Ade's parents, Mr. and Mrs. Babalola, who were in their mid-eighties. They had seen many years of public service, and were now retired. Beside Ade, there was no child in the big house. Six of their children had left home. Ade was the remaining child. His parents were very reluctant to let him go. They felt his absence would throw them into an abysmal solitude. Ade had been eager to break that umbilical cord, but his parents would not let him. However, he had made up his mind that as soon as he got a job, he'd leave home. "They can whine all they want," Ade said. "I'm tired of their trying to born me again."

Ike discovered that the old people were nice and very kind. They found Ike to be a pleasant, sensible, and forward-looking young man. He and their son were about the same age, around twenty-three.

CHAPTER 32

The first rain of the year came today, March 27th, 1932, and it was a heavy down pour accompanied by lightening and cracking thunderstorm. When such rain falls, villagers say the heaven's gate might have been left open.

Trees and thatched roofs were blown down by violent storm. Plants and shrubbery reclined in obedience to the crushing windstorm. Powerful floodwater created big gullies, and potholes, rendering the village footpaths almost impassable. Floods of rain-water settled in deep pool of water wherever they could hold together, the rest rushed into the nearest river. The story was the same across Ifite.

That day, Emeka was in the farm. Adaego had warned him that the first rain of the year usually came with thunderstorm and lightening and that he should always watch the sky and must begin to head home before the rain started. Emeka was in the farm doing some clearing in preparation for the next planting season. Other villagers had also started clearing their fields.

Oliaku often accompanied Emeka to the farm, but today she went to Eziagulu to visit her grandmother. She assisted Emeka to do many assignments. She was very helpful to the family where she now belonged after escaping from Nzom with Ike.

This was the second time she had paid her grandmother a homely visit. In the first visitation, her grandmother and all members of her family received her with great joy. They celebrated her victorious escape from Nzom. They gave her many presents and nicknamed her *Omeka nwoke* (bravery like a man), or a heroine. Young men, chiefs, and wealthy natives, were vying to marry her.

Oliaku had recently started primary school at the behest of Ike who also paid her school fees. Initially, she refused to go to school, saying that she was too old to carry slates and chalk. Besides, she did not know what the teachers were talking about. But Ike wrote back from Lagos and insisted she must go to school. He told her she'd enjoy school when she began to understand what was being taught. After much pressure, Oliaku started school. She was, however, pacified when she saw pupils as old as she was in the class.

Meanwhile, Emeka had almost rounded up his work in the farm when the heavens broke loose. The rain didn't give warning. It came all too sudden. Instead of taking shelter in his shanty, as most farmers did, he decided to brave the rain. He claimed he did not know when the rain would stop and that he didn't want to stay in the farm waiting indefinitely.

He came back drenched and cold. His mother was sympathetic.

"You must remove those wet clothes immediately and go to the fire place to warm yourself, you don't want to catch cold" Adaego told him. But Emeka kept opening one pot after another in search of food. He was hungry.

"Sure, but I need to wash first," Emeka said with his mouth full.

"Wash?" Adaego asked in disbelief. "When you are already shaking with cold? I can't understand. Hasn't the rain washed you clean enough?

"The rain beat me but did not wash me," Ike replied depositing himself on a kitchen stool to attack a bowl of yam porridge.

"Suit yourself," Adaego retorted. "Only make sure you didn't catch cold. There's nobody here to take care of you if you get sick. When you have eaten, come and get your letter."

"My letter? Who wrote me?"

"Do I know?"

Emeka wondered who had written him. It must be Ike, he thought. Who else would write me?

When he had finished his meal, he tore the envelope. Alas, it was Ike as he guessed. He found five pounds in the letter. He jumped up ecstatically. He ran inside with the money and threw everything on his mother's lap. "Ike wrote the letter."

"Oh, Ike my son," Adaego cried. She picked up the piece of paper ignoring the money.

"See the money in it," Emeka reminded her.

"Emeka I saw it, but let me see my son's letter first."

"You are only looking at your son's letter, not your son himself, not even his photograph. You can't even read the letter, can you?" Ike teased his illiterate mother. "Nne, you're holding the letter upside down."

"Which do I know?" she laughed and threw the piece of paper back to Emeka. "Read it for me."

Of the five pounds in the letter, Ike instructed that three pounds should go to Emeka and Oliaku for their school fees and books; one pound to their mother; and five shillings each to himself and Oliaku for their pocket money.

That was how Ike shared his income. He sent money to his family occasionally for their school needs and food. Since Ike started work, Emeka had no problem paying his school fees. Ike made sure his brother got his school fees on time. Emeka never suffered the humiliation of lacking school fees, books, and uniforms as Ike did during his primary school days. Ike had sworn that his brother would never go through the hardship he went through in order to acquire education.

The financial support Ike sent home enabled the family to feed well. Occasionally, they provide meat in the menu. Meat was a luxury they or anybody couldn't afford all the time. Most of the time, they cooked with small fish, crayfish, or mushroom. These days however, with the occasional windfall from Ike, they ate meat. Oliaku loved meat so much. Any day they had meat in the menu, she flaunted around fatuously like a little poppy. And she'd perform all the house chores with dispatch. And Emeka would tease her,

"When there is meat in the graters, women go extra miles in their chores."

And Oliaku would giggle,

"I don't care what you say, I love meat."

Since Ike started work, things had taken a better turn for the Anierobis.

In the letter he wrote, he said he'd update their old house. The thatched roof was caving in. He said he'd roof the house with zinc sheets, as against the thatch sheet. This way, the roofing would remain permanent, no more periodic renewal. Adaego was highly excited. She would probably be the first person to have such a luxury in the village.

"My son to provide me with zinc roofing," she said to herself out of joy, "may I live to see it happen. If the Almighty God says that the poor will live, the poor will indeed live. In the sight of God, nothing is incomprehensible."

In her reply, Adaego thanked Ike for all the money he sent her. "Tell him," she dictated to Emeka, "that I heard his promise about the zinc roofing, and that I'm looking forward to it. However, remind him that the important thing to me is his well-being; that God may keep him alive.

"Tell him he should not worry so much about us. He should look after himself to ensure his good health. Things are not too bad here as it was in the past. Tell him that we are fine."

Emeka paused and stared at her mother incredulously trying to manipulate the local dialect into an intelligible

English language without any harm to their own wellbeing. He was not satisfied with the last dictation. He was wondering how to structure this paragraph so that Ike would not believe that they were okay and stop sending money.

"We are fine you say?" he asked skeptically.

"Yes, are we not?" Adaego replied, not quite sure of herself. "Things are relatively better now, aren't they?"

"Well, I'm afraid if you say things are fine with us and that he should stop worrying about us, he might stop sending us money, do you know that?" Emeka pointed out chewing the end of his pen.

Adaego stared at her son in confusion and then looked at the sheet of paper in front of her. She wondered if she had actually dictated something detrimental to their course. Have I said the wrong thing? she thought as she looked blank.

"Emm... My son, you should know how to put the message together to make sense, Ike will understand. He is not a child. I mean, he should manage his resources well, and must not neglect his own needs because of ours. I didn't say he should stop helping us. *If I used a male goat to make reference, did I say the lion should snatch it?* I don't want him to feel that we are still dying of hunger as before. He should not starve himself for our sake. You should know how to balance the two ideas."

Emeka nodded his head satisfactorily and wrote on.

CHAPTER 33

Since Ike left home, he had not heard from Nneka, neither had Nneka heard from him. They lost contact. Nneka was transferred again from Port Harcourt to Onitsha. But Ike was not aware of this. He had written Nneka several times with her old address thinking that she was still at Port Harcourt. He never got a reply.

Nneka assumed Ike refused to write her because his attention was now diverted to the young woman he brought from *ofesi* (across the river). She heard everything about Ike's ordeal; from his fishing expedition at Okuiyi Ngene, to his escape from captivity with a girl who made his get-away possible. Most likely he'll marry the girl, Nneka thought.

Although Ike brought a girl from Nzom, Nneka was still nursing the hope that one day she and Ike would get married and live together. She often wondered if the girl from Nzom had captured his heart. Does he love her? she always surmised. Ike might have fallen in love with this rustic lass because of her kindness in saving his life. She deserves it any way, Nneka judged.

She admitted that the best way Ike, or anyone else, would reward somebody who made such a sacrifice, would be to marry the individual. This possibility disturbed Nneka a great deal. It kept her miserable. She did not want to lose Ike to anybody.

What's more, there was another *wood in the furnace -* Angela. Angela had Ike's child. Nneka thought that Ike might eventually be persuaded by his people to marry Angela because of the child Ike had with her. Nneka figured that her chances of having Ike were slim, compared with those of her two contenders. Piecing these circumstances together, she arrived at a conclusion that she was the least qualified among the three of them.

Despite the thorns and thistles that lay on her path to her goal, Nneka was determined to continue to tread this path. She loved Ike with a demanding possessiveness and she knew that Ike loved her too. He had given her a firm promise, time without number. Therefore, she was determined to fight the battle to the end. She did not want to give up. Women's love is sticky. They do not give up easily. They will continue to fight; they will continue to hope; and they will continue to hang on.

Whenever Nneka remembered this complex issue, her heart sank. She felt some invisible burden. She did not want to lose Ike in her life. Ike or nobody, she often told herself. At times while meditating over this knotty problem, she became depressed. Her fears were genuine because her contenders had good resumes. She had nothing to her credit except love.

CHAPTER 34

Angela's child, Ikechukwu Jr. (Angela named him after his father), was waxing stronger every day. He'd be four years in a couple of months. He was a healthy looking child and shared a lot of features with Ike. They said that Ikechukwu junior was a carbon copy of his father. Ike had not seen the child since he was born.

From time to time his mother, Adaego, talked about this child. She often remarked that the child *was a dropping in a remote land*. She was desperate to have him. Left to her, the child and his mother should be brought to her home.

Ike did not want the child nor his mother. He hated to be associated with that shameful incident at Onitsha. He wished it didn't happen. He wanted Angela to marry someone else and to take the child with her. But the Igbo culture does not work that way.

At present, the young Ikechukwu was with his grand parents at Onitsha. He was a cute little boy and they were very fond of him. When Angela was pregnant with the child, she did not want to have him. If she had her choice then, she would terminate the pregnancy. But now she loved the boy to death. She said the young Ike was the best thing that had happened to her. She loved Ike senior to the bone and often saw him through the lenses of Ike junior.

Angela had completed her secondary school and had entered a nursing school, a career she cherished.

CHAPTER 35

Ike was fast adjusting to Lagos life. He was happy working in the Peoples Bank as a clerical staff. He was also earning a good salary. He never thought he could earn such a handsome pay in his life. Banks are among the companies that pay very well. It was prestigious too to work in a bank. Not everybody could be that lucky to secure a bank-job. Ike counted himself very lucky. He did not have anybody to speak for him, but he got the job. The home folks would say: *The gods ward off menacing flies for a tailless cow.* Ike now saw himself climbing the ladder of success.

At Lagos, he felt very much at home with the Babalola family. The old couple took him as one of their sons and gave him parental treatment. Beside shelter, the Babalolas fed Ike and provided him with all the things he needed.

On his part, Ike assisted the old people in their needs. He performed chores and ran errands for them. He was always available whenever the old folks needed his help. He seldom went out with Ade who was always on the move, like the Yorubas, attending parties and social events. Ike stayed and played with the old couple, and they came to cherish his company. He listened to their life stories which they told over and over again without remembering they had done so before.

Ike and his friend, Ade, went to work every day at the Peoples Bank located at Ikeja. The two friends liked their new job. Ike's performance was outstanding. While his colleagues were still trying to find their feet in the new job, Ike was already making progress. He even treated difficult tasks that were handled by older hands. He worked as if he had been in the job for many years. His performance began to attract attention. He impressed everybody including the Manager.

Because of his outstanding performance, Ike's boss, Mr. Benjamin Abayomi, took particular interest in him. He discovered that Ike had great talents and creativity. What is more, he went extra mile in performing his duties.

When there was a need to meet a deadline, Ike stayed behind after the regular work hours. He did so even when the job did not attract overtime compensations. This thrilled the higher officers and they were interested in him.

In no time, Ike's proficiency became known throughout the institution. Barely six months after he started work, he had become the darling of the executive members of the company. Everybody knew Ikechukwu Anierobi. It was already muted that he might be picked to attend the four-year staff development training. The opportunity for this training program was awarded only to hardworking, efficient, and intelligent young men and women who had proved their worth in the service of the company. The award was strictly on merit.

Ike's boss had confessed that he had never seen a worker with Ike's glamour. Mr. Abayomi, a fastidious and meticulous pundit who could hardly be pleased, confessed that Ike's proficiency and skills were fascinating. He told his fellow Managers in an executive meeting that this young man was simply "ingenious and exceptional." He said that Ike's accomplishment was unique and that he had never seen a devoted worker like him in his 25 years of banking service.

Customers preferred Ike to serve them because he was quick, scrupulous, and accurate. He smiled at customers, and remembered their names, even those he met only once.

One day an elderly lady, one of Ike's regular customers, came to the bank to do business. Unfortunately Ike was away on tour with the Manager. Sikiratu, a staff, who sat next to Ike, wanted to help the old woman, but the woman turned down the offer and went home. She came back another day and was glad to see Ike.

Stories about his incandescent performance had reached distant shores. The Managing Director, Mr. Bode Williams, had heard about Ike. The MD, a pragmatic executive functionary, never delayed to compensate his staff for exceptional performance. At the same time, he did not waste time to punish an offender. A short man with bald patch, his workers often said that Mr. Williams had *a bowl of honey on one hand, and an axe to grind on the other*. When the news about Ike reached him, he promoted Ike far above what people expected.

CHAPTER 36

As expected, Ike was one of the few lucky workers that were selected to attend the four-year staff Development Training at Yaba College of Technology, Lagos. Six months after their graduation, the candidates were ready for posting. Of all the staff who attended the Training in the country, Ike got the best result.

There were twelve branches of Peoples Bank in Nigeria. Six of them needed Managing Directors. Only four Managers were available to fill the vacant posts. Ike was one of them. Unbelievable!

One Manager was to proceed to the Eastern Region, one to the Northern Region, and two to the West.

Onitsha was a busy commercial city and a good place for banking business. The Peoples bank at Onitsha was not making progress. The output was poor considering the volume of business in the city. The national executive board of Peoples Bank Lagos had noted that the company was not tapping enough of the resources at Onitsha and they needed a competent manager there.

There were altogether twenty-five employees at the Onitsha branch. Alfred Anierobi, Ike's cousin, happened to be one of them. He had worked with the bank for several years, and had risen to the rank of Executive Officer. The position of EO was five levels before the post of Managing Director. Senior staff hierarchy was as follows: Executive Officer, Senior Executive Officer, Manager, Deputy Director, and lastly Managing Director.

A nagging problem at the Onitsha Branch of Peoples Bank was the in-fighting among the senior staffers. The Managing Director, Mr. Chidume Onyekwelu, an arduous but a laissez-faire executive, had problem controlling his work force. The situation was adversely affecting progress in the bank. He was also corrupt.

Time and again inspectors were detailed from Lagos to sort things out, but matters never got better. Each time the inspectors came to Onitsha, they spent a lot of time settling disputes among the staff. When things got out of control, the headquarters saw the need for a more efficient leadership in this branch.

At the heat of this feud, a memo came from Lagos stating that a new Managing Director was coming to replace the incumbent Director. The message also revealed that the new Director had the directives to revamp and transform the staff structure. He also was given the mandate to fire and hire.

. Following this information, the employees at Onitsha were rattled. They were afraid of layoffs. No one knew upon whom the axe would fall. They crossed their fingers and waited in fear.

A week later it was rumoured that the new Managing Director was in town. Arrangement was underway to receive him. The atmosphere was tense. The new MD had made contacts with the incumbent Director, Mr. Onyekwelu, about his arrival at Onitsha. They had scheduled his first familiarization meeting with the staff.

A conference to receive the new man was scheduled for next Monday at 10:00 a.m. It was planned that after the general meeting, the big boss from Lagos would hold an exclusive meeting with the senior staff members.

Mr. Onyekwelu had since completed arrangements for a smooth handover. Workers had heard rumours that the incoming Managing Director was an assiduous, dynamic, and no-nonsense executive. They heard he did not take kindly to indolent, inefficient, and slipshod workers. The rumours made everybody to sit up even before the new MD took office. Some senior staff made frantic efforts to get their records straight. Workers struggled tirelessly to clear the back-log of work on their tables.

CHAPTER 37

On Monday, the employees of Peoples Bank were early to arrive in the office. Nobody was late, not even Mrs. Nkemdirim Igboanugo, the habitual late-comer.

The conference room had received a face-lift. The previous week, it was decorated with ribbons and flowers for the arrival of the new Managing Director. Everybody was anxious to meet the man.

There were two executive chairs kept at the high table, one for the outgoing MD, the other for the new MD. Ten yards away from the high table were armchairs lined up at the side of the wall for the senior officers. In the middle of the hall were rows of chairs for the rest of the staff. The meeting was mandatory; besides, everybody wanted to meet the new MD.

At 9:45 a.m., all employees were seated. Also, the senior staff members were on their seats. The hall was bussing with conversation by workers who were full of nervousness and expectations.

At one minute to ten, Mr. Onyekwelu walked into the hall side-by-side with a tall handsome man in his late twenties. All eyes were focused on him. He was the cynosure of everybody in the conference room. He walked slowly in short steps nodding his head to some comments the outgoing MD was making. People were expecting someone advanced in age, but this man was quite young, vibrant, and colourful. He was dressed in a dark suit looking very executive and vivacious. He had a black tie on a sparkling white shirt. His shoes were jet-black. He commanded great personality.

The hall was quiet. Since the man entered the conference room. An animated smile was sitting on his lips. Many workers wished that the smile would remain on his face and also in his heart as long as he stayed with them. Young women sitting at the back rows were busy doing some analysis of the new officer. They were enchanted by his good looks and personality features. He was handsome and had a captivating carriage.

"I have never seen such a specimen of manhood," said one of the girls

"That's right, he has flawless features as far as I know," admitted another lady.

"Is he married?" a third lady asked.

"Why do you ask?" another woman said. "You're already married and old."

"I know, but my daughter is not," she replied and hitched up her bra.

They laughed quietly, shielding their mouths.

When the two men got to the table, Mr. Onyekwelu beckoned the new DM to a seat. All eyes were focused on the new officer. A spell of unraveled charisma hung around his imposing personality. He looked everything business. Workers predicted that the man who would end the internal wrangling among the employees had arrived. They could tell he possessed the faculty to steer the wheels of progress to a dynamic course.

The man exuded, attraction, vivacity, and youth. His outfit was excellent and no match to Mr. Onyekwelu's jacket that had seen many years of washing and ironing.

Mr. Onyekwelu cleared his throat, adjusted his tie, and said,

"Good morning ladies and gentlemen. All of you know that today is a special day for us in this branch of the Peoples Bank. Today we have an august visitor who will soon become part of this organization. May I introduce to you the new Managing Director of the Peoples Bank Onitsha? Please welcome Mr. Ikechukwu Anierobi."

The new man rose from his seat. He smiled to the audience, nodded his head, and sat down.

At the mention of the name "Anierobi" Alfred Anierobi, who was sitting among the senior staff members, said in his heart, what a coincidence, our new Managing Director has my name. A staff sitting next to him bent over and whispered,

"That's your namesake Fred."

"Sure, that's my namesake," Alfred responded gleefully, ignorant of who the new MD was.

As you all know," Mr. Onyekwelu continued, "Mr. Anierobi will be taking over the management of this bank. He will be your new Managing Director. I've not met Mr.

Anierobi before, but from what I heard about him, he is a brilliant, diligent, skillful, and hardworking gentleman. He is a graduate of Yaba College of Technology. We had a report that he graduated with the best result in that school. He is very erudite and has an incredible wealth of experience in the banking business.

"Mr. Anierobi is a charismatic and dynamic individual with an incisive mind. He is reputed for precision, accuracy, and acceleration. He is an exemplary moving force in the Peoples bank. And I must warn you, everybody must brace up to meet Mr. Anierobi's pace, for he moves very fast.

"A benign and understanding boss, Mr. Anierobi is a very nice man. He is humane and down-to-earth. I believe you will find him not only a dependable leader, but also a modest and supportive boss who will always be responsive to your problems. You'll enjoy working with Mr. Anierobi."

After his introductory speech, Mr. Onyekwelu asked the new MD if he had anything to say. The man stood up.

People were full of expectations about what he was going to tell them. They had been looking for a messiah and wondered if one had come. They heard he was tough. They were unsure what he had in stock for them – bread and butter or axe and sword?

Many workers at the Peoples Bank Onitsha had not been promoted since they started work because Lagos had frozen all promotions and benefits. The reason being that the bank wasn't living up to expectations. It had been going through many years of regression and losses. At a point, there was fear of layoff. But now, the employees felt that a messiah had come. They hoped that things would change with the new administrator. But there was still fear of retrenchment.

Addressing the workers, the new Managing Director said,

"I am pleased to be here today. Onitsha had been my home until I left several years ago for Lagos. Since then, I have been with the Peoples bank in Lagos. I'm glad to be back to Onitsha. I sincerely hope that we can work together to achieve the objective for which all of us are here. Together we can strive to improve the status of this branch of the Peoples bank.

"I believe we can achieve success if we work as a team," he continued, one hand in his pocket the other resting on the table. "As the saying goes, *when all hands join together, they can kill a fly.* We will need each other's corporation and support to achieve our goal. No man is an island. I don't have much to say for now. I only want to express my profound enthusiasm in meeting you, and also to pledge that I'm fully prepared to work with you if you are ready to work with me. As time goes on, we will come to know ourselves better. Thank you."

Towards the end of the conference, Mr. Onyekwelu began to introduce his senior staff to the new Managing Director. When he introduced Alfred Anierobi, the name rang a bell to the new MD. At the mention of Anierobi, he looked twice at Alfred and recognized him right away despite his bushy beard and worn out face. He smiled at Alfred and shook his hand a bit longer than he did other hands. Without disclosing himself, he talked to Alfred for a few seconds like a familiar person and moved on. Alfred did not recognize the MD, neither did he or any other person understand the reason why the new man held his hand longer than other hands. However Alfred attributed the gesture to their similarity in name.

Ike remembered that Alfred had secured a job in a bank at Onitsha years ago. However, he did not know it was Peoples Bank.

Ike knew pretty well that, despite his physical changes, the man he saw today was his cousin with whom he grew up at Onitsha years ago when he was an apprentice boy.

What a twist of fate, he thought, as he shook hands with the rest of the senior staff. What a turn of event! What a strange world!

Describing this turn of events, the home folks would say that *tomorrow is pregnant, and no one knows what it will bring forth.* This must be the reason why some wise people tread the path of life warily, for things may change in the future. Someone said: *While the day is still ending, its events have yet to be concluded.* Would these wise sayings be more applicable to Ike and Alfred's circumstance? Or would the Biblical declaration that: *"The first shall be the last and the last first"* be more appropriate in this great turn of events?

Alfred and Ike had not met since they left Ufele's house several years ago. Their meeting today was coincidental. They had both attained tremendous physical changes. Their physical transitions over the years were so much that Alfred did not recognize Ike, his cousin, even after his first and last names were mentioned during the introduction.

He thought it was just a mere coincidence. On Ike's part, when Alfred's name was mentioned, he recognized him despite his receding hair and aging features.

Alfred looked older than his age. He had gained a lot of weight and had a protruding belly. He was tall and huge like his father, Ufele.

Ike had also attained some physical changes. He looked great with a tremendous personality physique. He was a perfect example of physical fitness. He was clean shaved and had a nice haircut. He looked very handsome in his dark suit towering above like Alfred, but not as heavy. The family had a genetic endowment of great heights.

It never crossed Alfred's mind that the new Managing Director was his cousin, Ike, who was an apprentice trader under his father years back. There was no way he could've imagined that this man was the very Ike he called an indolent boy during their heated argument over a biology textbook. Alfred didn't know that the new MD was the very Ike he was asking: "what do you know in my biology text book?"

When Ike was working on getting his General Certificate of Education, Alfred did not know. Alfred did not know that after Ike left Onitsha following his expulsion from Ufele's business, and after his unfortunate ordeal at Nzom, he went to Lagos in search of a job. He got a job with the same Peoples bank at the Lagos headquarters and had worked for several years.

Furthermore, Alfred had no idea that Ike did the Staff Development Training at Yaba College of Technology which hoisted him to the leadership pinnacle. The program was equivalent of the first degree. Only the bright workers who proved their mettle were given the opportunity to attend the staff development training. The training gave beneficiaries direct inroad to the top management cadre.

When they were young, Alfred was completely unaware of what was going on in Ike's life. He knew nothing about Ike and Emeka and their solo life-struggle. Alfred did not visit Ike's mother who was bedridden. He had no familial relationship with that family, now or in the past. As a result, he was ignorant of the changes that came later in Ike's life.

The only history about this family that came readily to Alfred's mind was that Ike made a young student pregnant, and was consequently thrown out of his father's service. He believed that after his expulsion from business at Onitsha, Ike loafered away in the village with villains and miscreants, and that in one of his dare-devil activities, was caught stealing and was killed. That was all the account Alfred could give about Ike. He believed that Ike had died long ago following his captivity at Okuiyi Ngene. He had very bad feelings about Ike and could go to any length in castigating his name.

CHAPTER 38

Mr. Ikechukwu Anierobi, the new Managing Director, at the Onitsha branch of the Peoples Bank, had begun putting things in order. He was a fast and diligent worker. He was an accomplished winner who knew where he was going and how to get there. The Lagos authorities knew that Mr. Anierobi was equal to the task because he had done it before. After his graduation from Yaba College of Technology, he was detailed to reform an ailing bank at Sokoto, Northern Nigeria, as an Assistant Managing Director. He did the same transformation at Ilorin and Benin City respectively. Now they placed the Onitsha problem unto his shoulders.

Eight weeks after he resumed duty at Onitsha, Mr. Ikechukwu Anierobi had begun a massive reorganization of the moribund financial institution. During the course of his investigations, he discovered many irregularities, fraud, and redundancy.

The previous administration hired many people including unskilled and inexperienced workers.

Recruitment galore had continued until the law of diminishing returns clicked in. The bank was struggling under the weight of superfluous staffing. A huge amount of money was spent on bonuses and rewards. He discovered traces of embezzlements, double-dealings, and bribery.

This notwithstanding, the new MD decided not to retrench workers nor demote anybody. He was aware that the employees had dependants. If they were thrown out of job, many families would suffer; many mouths would go hungry; and many children would drop out of school. He was a compassionate man.

His plan was to make effective use of the excess workforce. He made his plan known to the workers in his subsequent conferences, and they were delighted that nobody would be sent away. However, he warned that everybody must sit up and get prepared to work at his pace. The workers were willing to stick with him as long as they retained their jobs.

Forthwith, the new MD sent a proposal to Lagos seeking permission to establish a new sub-branch of Peoples bank at Enu-Onitsha, with a long-term plan to open yet another branch at Odakpu. That way, all the workers would be absorbed in the new branches. He knew the proposal would work perfectly well when implemented because he had a good knowledge of Onitsha town where he grew up.

Onitsha was a big commercial center bustling with population. Merchants, traders, artisans, civil servants and businessmen, from different parts of Nigeria, made the commercial town one of the busiest in Africa. Mr. Ikechukwu Anierobi was aware of these geographical and demographic facts. He believed that Onitsha was a city whose commercial fabrics could absorb many banking establishments.

As time went by, things began to move faster and faster. Mr. Anierobi was a habitual fast worker and a goal-getter. The entire staff was moving along with him in his overhauling strategies. They rallied around him in his resuscitation program. Nobody lost his or her job; nobody lost promotion; nobody lost his or her benefits. Workers' amenities were restored again; overtime was restored; the pension scheme was restored. The bank was thriving. Employees couldn't be happier.

Within a short time the bank began to make outstanding progress. There was profit galore. The excess staff was absorbed in the new branch and plans were underway to establish another branch. Everybody was amazed at the pace at which things were moving. Everybody was on board the MD's vehicle of reform and reorganization except one man - Alfred Anierobi, his cousin.

At first, Alfred did not know that the new Managing Director of the Peoples Bank was Ike his cousin until one day when he came to the Director's office with his immediate boss to discuss some important fiscal matters.

The MD looked at Alfred and said, "I'm sure you do not recognize me. Do you remember who I am?"

Alfred looked at the Director bashfully trying to think. "I...I can't remember Sir," he said courteously. "We may have met somewhere. Really, you look familiar Sir."

Alfred's boss, Mr. Unegbu, was listening and smiling.

"Well, this is Ike your cousin," the Managing Director said.

"Sir, which Ike?" said Alfred nervously.

"Ikechukwu Anierobi, your cousin, who lived with you at Onitsha, years ago, when I was an apprentice boy under your father Ufele."

Immediately, Alfred's eyes opened and he recognized Ike. Jesus! he said in his heart. Mighty heavens! He was speechless. Instead of shouting for joy at the big surprise, he recoiled and was withdrawn. His face changed, but he feigned to be delighted. The MD and Mr. Unegbu could read his heart via his countenance despite his deceptive affect. They saw the bitterness and disappointment in his face. He was psychologically traumatized at this revelation. It was a shocker. He couldn't talk or move from his seat. He began to sweat.

Could this be true, Alfred thought. Ike is the Managing Director. I thought he died. How come? Yes, I can recognize him, but how can? How can such a thing happen on earth? I thought he was dead…What a disgraceful turn of event! What an irony! What a quirk of fate! How can this be, and how can the story be told? How can this happen and how can one believe it? Ike is the Managing Director, many levels of positions above me. Good gracious! This is incredible! This is unbelievable. This is…

Alfred was so frustrated and grossly disenchanted that he was unable to participate in the conference any more. He managed to grope his way out of the DM's office after the meeting.

Since that revelation, Alfred was not himself. His world seemed to have crashed. He was heartbroken. He became demoralized and browbeaten. He was bitterly envious.

It was obvious that he was still harboring that childhood ill-feelings he held against his cousin, Ike, when they were young. That animosity and hatred he held against Ike when they lived together in Ufele's house, were still deeply engrained in his sub- consciousness. He had not forgotten anything.

With regards to his job, he hated his work now. He refused to acknowledge whatever reorganization that was going on in the bank. He hated the fact that someone he never thought could go to school was now a graduate of Yaba College of Technology and was the overall Managing Director of the Bank where he was working. What an irony!

CHAPTER 39

Alfred was so incredulous about Ike's progress that he set out to investigate the authenticity of his profile. To make sure that the new Managing Director was the very Ike he knew, he made contacts with some apprentice boys who served his father at the same time that Ike was serving.

He was doing this because he was still not convinced about his cousin's miraculous accomplishments. He had no reason to believe that this was true. He recalled that his father refused to send Ike to secondary school. How then did he acquire the secondary school education in the first place? Alfred was a confused man and terribly envious.

He went to his father. He believed his father would know more about Ike and what he later did with his life.

Ufele was in his sitting room chewing some fresh corn when Alfred arrived. He usually stopped by every now and then to see his parents.

"Good evening Sir," Alfred greeted his father deeping his hand into the bowl of roasted corn.

"Good evening my son," Ufele replied. "How are you?"

"I'm well."

"How is work?"

"Same old crab."

"I'm glad you came," Ufele said after emptying a cup of water. "I wanted to send for you to discuss a loan."

"Loan?"

"Yes. I want some money. I am expecting some goods from overseas. I need some quick cash."

"Here I am," Alfred said feebly as he sank into a chair. "But before the loan issue, let me ask you a question for which I have come here."

"What is it?"

"Did Ike, my cousin, ever go to a secondary school when he lived in our house or when he left Onitsha?"

"Why?" Ufele asked in bewilderment. "Why do you ask?"

"Just answer my question," Alfred said, a little irritated. Apparently, he wasn't ready to discuss details. He knew his father was unaware of the latest development at the Peoples Bank. Although Ufele heard that the Bank had a new Managing Director, but he certainly did not know who the new man was. Alfred did not want to be the one to tell him.

"Well, I would've thought you were in a better position to know the answer to that question. Aren't you?" Ufele replied looking at his son with disrespect. "Ike is your age-mate and your cousin too. All of you played together when he lived with me. I would think you should know his affairs better than myself. You should know whether he went to school or not. However, to address your question, there was a time Ike requested me to help him secure a job in the bank, ostensibly because I got a job for you in the bank. I told him that I couldn't possibly do that because he had no qualifications. He then pulled a G.C.E. certificate from his pocket and showed me. He claimed he studied at home, took the G.C.E. examinations, and passed all his papers.

"That's all I know about Ike and school. Whether he actually studied and passed the GCE, I don't know. All I can remember is that I told Ike that he should stop worrying about a white-collar job, and that he'd do marvelously well in the business world. In any case, I would not be surprised if Ike got the G.C.E. certificate because that boy was incredibly brilliant."

Ufele was ignorant of the fact that Ike got more than the G.C.E. later.

"Ike was smart," Ufele went on. "It could've been possible for him to study at home and passed the exams. He has the smartest brain I ever know. When he was in my house, I saw him all the time with books. He read a lot, even more than those who were in school. He probably read at home and…"

That's okay," Alfred interrupted. "You've answered my question." He got up and headed for the door.

"Why did you ask?" Ufele demanded looking at him in confusion.

"Never mind."

Piecing all the information he gathered together, Alfred arrived at a conclusion that the story about Ike's success wasn't a myth but a fact of life. He was now convinced that Ike actually got the G.C.E. by studying at home. He learned that while he was studying in the secondary school in those days, Ike was studying at home for his G.C.E and at the same time learning business. In his research, he also learned that Ike passed the GCE exams; went to Lagos in search of job; got employment at the Peoples Bank; worked for years; and later got a scholarship to study at Yaba College of Technology, Lagos.

Alfred now realized why Ike picked up his textbooks every now and then. He recalled an incident when he had a fight with Ike because Ike took his biology book without his permission. "Hmmmmm!" he sighed.

Instead of admiring his cousin for his astounding accomplishments, Alfred became embittered, resentful, and envious. He hated Ike. Undeniably, he was still harbouring the memories of his bad relationship with Ike. He wouldn't let go of his baseless animosity against his brother.

Following his discovery, and without any justifiable reason, Alfred began to nurse acrid hatred against Ike, wishing him evil. The more he thought about this turn of event, the more he became embittered. The acrimony he harboured against his cousin when they were teenagers revived in full force, this time in a more egregious fashion.

In the office, Alfred hadn't been himself since he discovered that the new Managing Director of the Peoples Bank was Ike, his cousin. He was not at peace with himself. Each time this matter came up in his mind, he felt sore. He said many unpleasant things about the new MD. His colleagues could not understand the basis for his ill-feelings against the new Managing Director whom they believed was a nice man and doing a great job.

Gradually Alfred began entertaining evil thoughts against the MD. He felt quite uncomfortable working under Ike. How can I live to work under him? he often wondered. How on earth can I take orders from this man?

Alfred vowed to do something to obvert this situation. He said he would not live to see Ike boss him. This can't happen in my life, he said to himself. He was sitting alone in his office soliloquizing. He did this all day at work. Over my dead body, he would say. Who is he? Who is Ike to boss me? I can't believe this. To hell with him! I must destroy… He stopped talking to himself when his door opened and someone walked in.

But the fact remained that Ike was his boss. All the tenants at No. 3 Ekwulobia Street had heard the new development at the Peoples Bank. Ufele had gone to the bank personally to verify the story, and it was true. The boy he denied all access to education years back, was now the Managing Director of the Peoples Bank Onitsha. All the apprentice boys who served Ufele had heard the story.

One day, one of them, Ejiofor, saw Alfred at the bank and said to him,

"I heard that Ike is now the Managing Director of the Bank?"

"Which bank?" Alfred retorted angrily, as if he did not know.

"The Peoples Bank, where you are working."

"I don't know about that," he replied bluntly.

"Do you mean you didn't know that Ikechukwu, your cousin, is the new Managing Director of the Peoples Bank where you are working?"

"If you are looking for Ike," said Alfred contemptuously, "go and look for him. Leave me alone."

Ejiofor got the message. A curious smile played on his lips when he realized that Alfred was bitter over Ike's life achievement. He wasn't surprised. He read discontent in his face as well as in his speech and said,

"The table has turned eh, Alfred."

"Look here man," Alfred said angrily, "I don't want any nonsense, you hear me!"

He left Ejiofor and went away muttering obscenities.

CHAPTER 40

In the weeks and months that followed, Alfred missed work several days leaving a back-log of work on his desk. He had since stopped participating in the bi-weekly senior staff meetings chaired by the Managing Director. He did all he could to avoid face-to-face contact with the MD. One day the MD sent for him for discussion following reports that Alfred was not doing his job. Alfred did not go. He asked the Director's secretary to say that he was sick.

Having sworn to deal with Ike, Alfred began a wicked plot to accomplish his objective. He decided that the best way to get over this ignominious turn of event was to kill Ike. He was ashamed because employees of the bank had become aware of his relationship with Ike as well as their background history. They heard that Alfred Anierobi and the new DM, Mr. Ikechukwu Anierobi, were cousins and that Alfred's father, Ufele, denied the young Ike education when he was a child. They heard how Ike was crying and begging for help to go to school; they heard how Alfred's father told Ike that he had no money to send him to school, and yet, he sent his own son, Alfred, to school; and they also heard how Ike later struggled to reach his present position through self-efforts. They heard everything about these two individuals, past and present.

Onitsha metropolitan city was a place where anything could be obtained provided you had the money. Thus, Alfred went underground looking for ways and means to accomplish his diabolical intent. It did not take him long to find a way.

He was introduced to a brigand called Akpunku, a hit-man. Akpunku was one of the notorious crooks Onitsha ever known. He made money by killing people on contract. He knew all the criminals and dare-devils in town. Akpunku was the man Alfred contracted to kill Ike.

In their first meeting, Alfred told Akpunku that he wanted him to kill the Managing Director of the Peoples Bank Onitsha.

"That's not a problem," Akpunku laughed in his habitual flippant way. They were alone during this secret meeting.

"I don't want anybody to know about this," Alfred stressed.

"That's not a problem."

Between his two fingers the hit man held a tiny stub of marijuana rap. He took the last puff, dropped the stub, and crushed it with his heel. "All I need is money. I need money to pay my boys. We don't accept checks. Cash only, raw cash! Before you close and open your eyes, the job is neatly done."

Alfred was excited. "Money is not a problem," he assured the man. "The problem is whether you are capable of executing the business without anybody knowing anything about it."

Alfred could hardly see the full image of the man he was talking to. The small underground room was dark. Except for a small transistor radio sitting on a wooden bench, and a small table between Akpunku and his host, there was nothing in this clandestine bunker.

"I want a clean job without any flaw or leak."

"You probably do not know who I am," Akpunku boasted, "otherwise you wouldn't be doubting the credibility of my business. If I were to reveal the jobs we had accomplished in the past, you wouldn't have any doubt in your mind about striking a deal with my company. However, for security reasons, we don't give samples.

"Why should you doubt me, Mr. Man?" Akpunku went on arrogantly, looking Alfred in the eye. "I have a force trained to abduct anybody on earth without the law enforcement knowing about it? If there is anybody I want to get today, my men can penetrate anywhere to take that person."

He guffawed loudly and packed his heavy legs on top the table and wrapped another weed.

CHAPTER 41

Because Onitsha was nearer home than Lagos, Ike visited the village almost every other weekend. The first day he visited home, the family was overjoyed. It was a memorable home-coming. He met his people sound in health. Adaego and Emeka were doing well, so was Oliaku, who had blended well with the Anierobi family. They had formed a closely-knit happy family.

Emeka and Oliaku were growing. Emeka had just completed his secondary school and was anxious to start work. Ike had promised to find him a job at Onitsha as soon as he finished secondary school.

Oliaku was looking very pretty. She had blossomed into a veritable young woman. Adaego liked her so much and had since made up her mind that one of her children must marry her. This speculation was buried deep in her heart. She did not want to share the thought yet.

Oliaku was on the verge of completing her primary school. That wasn't the appropriate age to be in a primary school, but she did not mind. It wasn't her fault. There were no schools at Nzom. At that time, the missionaries were only beginning to build elementary schools in the rural communities under their parish. Oliaku was delighted when Ike announced he'd sponsor her in the secondary school. She liked school now.

Oliaku was well treated by the members of Anierobi family. She still remembered her people though, especially her mother and her siblings. But she had no wish to go back to Nzom. She knew they would kill her. She was quite safe and happy at Ifite.

Adaego was enchanted by Ike's physical stature. "You look rather huge and terrifying." she said to him.

"You're right mother," Oliaku supported shyly, "Ike has changed a great deal. I can't believe he was the one."

"I bet he eats a lot of meat all day," said Emeka. "Look at his fat neck."

They all laughed.

They saw only the physical changes in Ike, they did not see the astounding career change of this man. They did not know how important Ike was now.

"I'm happy to see all of you looking good and healthy," Ike told them with an affectionate smile. "You all look great."

"Is it true you're now at Onitsha?" Adaego asked, a little incredulous.

"Yes," Ike replied.

"That's much better," she said. "I'm so happy. Onitsha is much nearer home than Lokos."

"It's Lagos, not Lokos," Emeka corrected his mother.

"I'm glad to be near home," Ike said, stroking his mother on the shoulder, "although there's much work to do at Onitsha."

"Is there really much work worth complaining about in pushing the pen?" Emeka wondered adjusting a small dinning table in front of his brother for the dinner. "That's no big deal, just writing."

"You'll soon start work," said Ike washing his hands, "by then, you will find out how difficult it is to push the pen. You think it's that simple?"

Oliaku looked at Emeka jealously. She wished she were the one getting ready to start work.

"This soup is delicious," Ike commented as they ate dinner. Everybody was around the table eating from the same bowl. "Who cooked the soup?"

"Me," Oliaku claimed hurriedly.

"Is that right? So you are a good cook, eh?"

"Don't listen to her," Emeka challenged. "She simply wanted to claim credit for it. The only soup she can cook is the one that runs down the elbow - *Ofe nsala* (pepper soup)"

There was a protracted laughter in the room. Everybody was choking. Oliaku was suffocating with laughter.

"I cooked the soup," Emeka claimed.

"Who guided you in the process?" Oliaku challenged with a chuckle. "Mother was directing you throughout, wasn't she?"

"Mother told me when to put what ingredient in the soup," Emeka agreed, "she never came to the kitchen. How about that?"

Ike looked at Emeka ludicrously. "The essential part of cooking is putting the ingredients at the appropriate time and at a requisite quantity. Putting ingredients in the pot at the behest of someone else is simply running cooking errand. Whoever that called for the timely application of the component parts of the soup was the actual cook. In that sense, mother was the cook."

Oliaku burst into another spate of laughter. They were having real fun and it was always like that.

CHAPTER 42

Ike and Nneka had lost contact for a long time. During one of his home visits, he went to Nneka's home to ask for her whereabouts. He learned that Nneka was right there at Onitsha.

When he got back to Onitsha, he went to see her. At the Ministry of Education, he went first to the Commissioner's office, Mr. Steve Nwasi, who happened to be his primary school mate. Earlier, the two gentlemen had met at the People's Bank after many years. Mr. Nwasi graduated from the University of Ibadan where he majored in Education. The two men talked at length about their school days.

Mr. Nwasi sent his secretary to find Nneka.

Nneka was busy writing a report due for submission in a few hours. She could hardly raise her head when Mary-Ann walked in.

"You can't even greet me, girl," Mary-Ann teased Nneka.

"Sorry my dear, I'm not ignoring you," Nneka replied. "I'm trying to finish this report. What's going on?"

"Somebody wants to see you in the Commissioner's office," Mary-Ann said.

Nneka looked at Mary-Ann with probing eyes. "In the Commissioner's office? Who's the person?" she asked nervously.

"I don't know."

Nneka stopped writing and stared at Mary-Ann with her brow knitted. "A man or a woman?"

"Hmmmm! question. A man."

"What's his name?"

Mary-Ann was getting bored. "Nneka, I have not taken my lunch. I don't have enough energy to answer these questions. The Commissioner did not tell me the man's name, but I think he said the man was the Managing Director of the Peoples Bank."

After that, Mary-Ann turned and left.

Nneka followed her to the door with her eyes, still wondering. Managing Director of the Peoples Bank, she said to herself, what have I got to do with the Managing Director of the Peoples Bank?

She got up and ran after Mary-Ann. When they got to the Commissioner's door, Mary-Ann bid her good luck and slid into her own office. Nneka wished that Mary-Ann would accompany her to the Commissioner's office.

Nervously she knocked at the door. "Come in," the Commissioner responded.

Gingerly Nneka turned the doorknob and saw a man in a black suit, looking highly dignified. Nneka did not know the individual. Her cautiousness exposed her nervousness.

Ike deliberately wore a serious look refusing to remove his sunglasses. He wanted to know if Nneka could recognize him. She couldn't.

Ike's physical features had greatly changed over the years. He and Nneka had not seen each other for many years. He had grown into a huge handsome man. He looked colourful and terrific in his black suit. He was a mountain of a man.

Who can this be? Nneka thought as she prodded forward timorously to receive the stranger's handshake. Ike maintained his composure and watched her reactions. The commissioner was watching the drama. Ike had earlier briefed Mr. Nwasi to withhold any introduction.

Ike tried to suppress a smile. "Do you still not recognize me?" he said as he removed his glasses. He was almost bursting with laughter.

"Jesus! Ike!" Nneka shouted. "Ike!" She leapt unto Ike's waiting arms. "Is this Ike? Oh my God! Oh gracious Lord! Ike, Ike, Ike. I can't believe this. Is this…? Heavens! This must be a dream. Is it real? Is it you Ike?"

"It's me," Ike smiled and hugged Nneka passionately. "How are you?"

Nneka was stunned. She took a few steps backwards, and studied the man. "Is this a dream or reality?"

She raced forward and dived into Ike's arms again. Her heart was filled with joy. She couldn't believe it wasn't one of those dreams in which she often met Ike with inexplicable joy, only to wake up to realize it was only a dream. This time it wasn't a dream, it was real. They were meeting in real life - she and the man she loved.

Nneka's joy was beyond description. Nothing was more important in her life than what was happening now. She heaved a sigh and sank into a chair looking at Mr. Ikechukwu Anierobi.

Ike, a bank Manager? she thought as she studied the very Ikechukwu she knew from primary school. How come? How did he manage? Am I to believe this or not? A bank Director? How did this come about? How did he start?

CHAPTER 43

Six months later, Ike and Nneka were almost ready to wed in the Church. Ike had completed the traditional marriage process. He had taken wine to Nneka's people and they accepted the wine. This is fundamental in Igbo customary marriage. The Ifite people now knew that Nneka Akigwe was the wife of Ikechukwu Anierobi. They blessed the marriage.

Next was the Church marriage. Nneka had looked forward to her wedding day. For the past few months she and Ike had been preparing for the wedding. Nneka was highly excited. That was exactly what she wanted in her life. Her dream had come true and she was going to the altar with the man she loved; the man she had been dying for; and the only man she wanted in her life. She couldn't be happier.

The love Nneka had for Ike was sticky. Despite all the bumps on the way, her love for this man could not change nor fade. To her, Ike was irreplaceable. She always thought about him, hoping that one day they would meet again.

And now, not only that they had met, they were about to get married.

"Who said that God does not answer prayers?" Nneka had told one of her friends. "I prayed about this, and He answered me."

Sometimes when she was alone, Nneka reminisced how her relationship with Ike started. What usually slithered across her mind was their brief meeting on the road, years ago, when she was returning from the river with a bucket of water, and Ike was going to the river. Nneka recalled how she stopped Ike and asked him why he hadn't been attending classes. Ike had replied that he was expelled for owing school fees. Nneka remembered that she later lent Ike some money to pay his school fees.

Today, while she was standing at the balcony of Ike's house at Onitsha, the same thought went across her mind. She began to wonder how events of life turn around. She wondered whether Ike still remembered these things that happened when they were children. He must have forgotten everything, she said to herself as she looked at the cobwebs at the joint of the balcony ceiling.

Shortly after, Ike joined her at the balcony. They were enjoying the fresh air and looking out at the trees that adorned the landscape of the Government Reservation Area. The balcony offered a scintillating panoramic view of the housing estate. The estate was the luxurious quarters of top civil servants, mainly white folks and very few black bureaucrats.

Nneka smiled graciously as Ike walked up to her. He did not realize why she greeted him with that glamorous smile.

He did not know the thoughts that were going through her mind at that moment.

As the couple talked about the wedding at the balcony, the cool evening breeze careered across their faces, reminding them of the most important day in their lives. Ike suddenly went inside the room and came out with a parcel and handed it to Nneka.

"What is that?" Nneka asked amazed.

"It's a gift for you, open it," Ike said with an affectionate smile.

Nneka hesitated. "A gift for me?"

"Yes, open it."

Nneka looked at Ike with deep-rooted passion. She began to unwrap the parcel. She was wild about this man. She loved Ike with all the nerves in her being.

Alas! it was a pack of gold set - necklace, earrings, bangles, ring, etc., made of African solid gold. Nneka screamed! She had never seen such a solid gold package. She shouted for joy. Her chief bridesmaid, Monica, who was in the next room, hurried out to know what was happening. Her slippers were slapping the floor, flip-flap flip-flap as she rushed out to the balcony.

"Monica see," Nneka held up the gold set.

"Wow!" Monica shouted, "This is it! This is it! Wonderful! Gold necklace, gold earrings, gold bangles, gold ring, gold everything. This is fantastic! It's special! I have never seen this type. Nne you're on top of the world."

"Oooooh," Nneka moaned, "I haven't seen the like before.

Monica turned to Ike, "You're a great man," she said and shook his hand. "I thought you had already bought everything she needed for the wedding."

"Exactly," Nneka agreed, "he had bought me three complete sets to choose from, and then this."

"This gold set represents a little token for something very special in my life," Ike said to his wife holding her hand, "It's a gift for something you did for me, if you can remember the past."

Monica was confused but Nneka was not. Nneka knew immediately what Ike was referring to. She had thought that Ike had forgotten it, but she found out now that the incident was still etching in his memory vault.

"Ike turned to Monica who was watching but did not understand, and said,

"Nneka is a wonderful woman. She made me what I am today. She must have told you the story."

Nneka discussed her personal life matters with Monica, but not this particular issue.

"Oh Ike, how can I express my gratitude to you?" Nneka said excitedly leaning on his shoulder. "How can I compensate for all the kindness you are showing to me? You have spent a fortune on this wedding just for me."

"I'm only beginning," Ike laughed. "I'm paying you back for your kindness to me."

"Paying me back you said?"

"Yes, because you did a lot to jump-start my life. Do you remember the day I was going to the river, and you were coming back home from the river with your bucket of water…?"

"Yes, I remember," Nneka interrupted, "why is this incident necessary now? You would've achieved your life's ambition any way, you're a genius."

Nneka adjusted her loose wrapper and tapped Ike by the shoulder most affectionately. She did not want to hear about this simple deed, and she was modestly disclaiming credit for Ike's success in life.

Monica was watching. She was still at loss. Ike turned to her and narrated the story - how Nneka helped him with his school fees at primary school, etc. After that, Monica understood the whole story.

"You're a special human being to have done this at that age," she told Nneka with a faint note of admiration. "How many children can do that? You're someone special Nneka. I can now understand why your husband was spoiling you with gifts and affection. You deserve it because you did something extraordinary."

"But he has paid me back in several ways," Nneka protested hugging Ike again.

"I haven't really started," Ike replied. "I'll continue to pay for this till I die."

"Oooooh! Ike, don't make me cry. Aren't you so sweet?" Nneka said and buried her face on his chest. Tears of joy were flowing. "I love you," she whispered to him through her tears.

"I love you too baby," Ike replied and kissed her mouth passionately.

"Ike, do you say I deserve all these?"

"You deserve them and more. You did something in my life that I can never forget. You are my Angel. You are my world, you are my life. That kindness will live with me forever, and as long as I remember it, so long will I continue to admire you, cherish you, and continue to pay you back for it."

Nneka was emotional. She was touched at the bottom of her heart by all the nice things Ike was saying to her. She wiped her tears with Ike's sparkling shirt. Joy filled her heart to realize that her simple childhood kindness was highly valued and appreciated.

She went to the mirror to try the necklace. She turned to Monica who was watching them swimming and submerging reminiscently in their wonderful past, "I wonder what I'll look like tomorrow."

"You'll look magnificent," Monica remarked. "You'll look like an Angel,"

They laughed aloud.

Monica was excited to be Nneka's chief bridesmaid, a portfolio she had never held before. She was Nneka's best friend since Nneka came to Onitsha on transfer. The two girls had been together since then. Monica was a rare good-natured individual. She was humble, nice, and well-behaved. She confessed she had never met a more loyal, dedicated, and dependable friend like Nneka. They called themselves "sister." They worked in the same Ministry of Education.

Monica was a tall figure and on the lean side. She was lithe and full of femininity. Her supple structure made her appear lethargic. Nneka once teased her, saying: "Are you sure this flexible frame of yours can hold the womb in place when the time comes?"

Nneka's wedding gown was terrific. Her friends described the gown as *One in town*. The marriage was only two days away. The wedding had been announced three times at St. Anthony's Catholic Church Fegge Onitsha. Relatives and friends of both spouses could not wait to celebrate the wedding. They had received the invitation.

The next day would be the bachelors' eve. The preparation was extensive. Ike was a popular figure. Even though he hadn't been too long in the city, his work as a Managing Director of a popular bank had put him on the limelight in the community. Many wealthy businessmen and top civil servants who did business with the Peoples Bank knew Mr. Anierobi very well. He was also an outgoing type. He honoured invitations for social events. It was, therefore, not surprising that many people were expected to attend his wedding.

CHAPTER 44

Ike's house was buzzing with activities. Everybody was busy putting things together for the wedding. Relatives were beginning to arrive from different places. Ike had a big house which his company allotted to him even before he arrived from Lagos.

Arrangements for the wedding were well underway. Guests, relatives, and friends had started to arrive in Ike's house. Visitors occupied every available space. One man's marriage in Igbo community is a celebration for all the villagers, especially if the bride and the bridegroom were wealthy. Everybody was invited, and many people were coming. Ike was an illustrious son.

Two buses were designated to convey villagers to Onitsha. The buses could not lift all that wanted to attend Ike's wedding. Those who could afford the fare, took public transportation.

Emeka and Oliaku had arrived a few days earlier. They didn't leave their mother by herself. Their aunt, Ifeatu, stayed with Adaego while they were away.

Oliaku had never been to any township. She was thrilled by all she saw at Onitsha - street lights, tall buildings, water running from pipe, tarred roads, cars, and lorries - everything. She saw white people too. She had never seen a white man in her life. She had heard that there were some human beings that had white skins. She saw them at Onitsha. She was fascinated with the city life. Emeka had told her about life in the city. Emeka had been to Onitsha a couple of times since Ike arrived from Lagos. Soon he'd leave the village permanently to live at Onitsha with his brother. He would also start work. That was certain. He had told Oliaku that some day she too would live in the city. Nothing had agitated Oliaku as this future arrangement. She looked forward to it.

In the evening before the wedding day, everywhere was bustling with activities in Ike's house. People went in and out of the building. Goods and consignments kept arriving. The three-bedroom duplex and the entire yard were buzzing with visitors. The population was so much that neighbours became involved. They received and squatted guests in their houses. Everybody knew the Managing Director, and everybody was willing to help.

All nooks and corners in Ike's house had been taken. During the night, visitors slept at veranda, balcony, and corridors. The Garage and kitchen were converted into bedrooms.

Ike had sent invitations to his former co-apprentice boys. They came. They had all grown and started their own businesses. Some were married, and they came with their wives. Successful ones were now rich. Even the imbecile "Mr. K" had made astounding development in his own business. While some of the boys settled at Onitsha after leaving Ufele's service, some moved to other cities like Aba, Enugu, Owerri, Benin, Sokoto Kaduna, Lagos, etc. The apprentice boys knew about Ike's progress. They were in touch with Ufele's family. It was a happy reunion for the old boys - THE APPRENTICE BOYS. Ufele and his wife, Akuoma, were also in attendance.

Oliaku was highly excited when she arrived at Onitsha with Emeka. That was the first time she rode in a motor vehicle. The awkward way she looked at people and at things was indicative that she had never seen any place. Earlier when she and Emeka arrived at Ike's house, she was climbing the stairs gingerly and cautiously as though the structure might collapse under their weight. She had never seen a storied building. Any time she looked down from the window, she was afraid of falling off. It was a titillating experience for her.

"Suppose this structure collapses?" Oliaku asked Emeka who was sitting on a sofa leafing through Ike's album.

"Collapse?"

"Yes."

"No, it can't collapse," Emeka explained. "It was built with iron, hard concrete, and cement. And it was built on a solid foundation. It's not a mud building like we have in the village."

Oliaku was pacified.

Downstairs, she saw groups of young men and women drinking. "What are these people up to?" she asked Emeka.

Each time she saw something that enticed her, she'd want to know what it meant.

Emeka came to the window and looked out. "The people are here for the wedding," Emeka explained. "They are getting ready for the bachelors' eve."

"What is bachelors' eve?"

"It means celebrating the last day of being single."

"What?"

"The day a man and a woman bid goodbye to single life. Do you understand?"

"No."

"O Lord. Bachelors' eve is part of the wedding process. Bachelors' eve precedes the actual wedding. It's the day a bachelor and a spinster shed the garb of bachelorhood and spinsterhood and slide into married life. The ceremony for this changeover is called bachelor's eve and is attended, in most part, by young men and women, who will one day get married too. Soon music and dancing will begin here, and we will go downstairs to enjoy the evening. Can you dance?"

Oliaku looked at Emeka and shook her head with a chuckle.

Ike had been busy all day receiving visitors who came from different places. He was exhausted. "I hope this event is over so we can have some rest," he spoke to Nneka who was checking the outfits for the flower girls.

"Yes darling," Nneka replied offering him a cup of soft drink. "Until now, I didn't realize that preparation for a wedding was such a demanding task, gush!"

"You don't know how big an undertaking is until you get into it."

"Thank goodness, it's once in a lifetime," Nneka said putting a small piece of fried meat into Ike's mouth. Monica had passed some nibbling to her a minute ago.

"Yes darling," Ike agreed, "that's one good thing about a wedding. It's a one-time event. We're not going to do this again. Did you show Raph the beer and other drinks?"

"Yes, he saw the drinks and okayed the quantity."

"That's good. I was thinking that we didn't have enough. I know that our people drink a lot of beer. Besides, the population out there is outrageous. I have never seen such a crowd. Did you anticipate we would have such attendance in our wedding love?"

"No sweetie," Nneka replied. "I never dreamed that my wedding could pull such a crowd. It's only because of your status and popularity."

"You are popular too. I just hope the drinks are enough."

"The man in charge of drinks, Raph Mmoneme, is experienced. When your friend, Bernard Ezeobu wedded, he was in charge of drinks. So I have no fears."

Ike and Nneka were still talking when Raph walked in and announced that the drinks would not be sufficient.

"I said it," Ike noted and rose from his seat. "I was just telling Nneka that the drinks might not be sufficient because the population out there was astonishing."

"Yes, there are many people in attendance," Raph agreed. "I took a second look at the crowd and felt we had better get more drinks. I have never seen such a crowd in a single wedding. It's better to be on the safe side. More drinks are needed."

Ike gave orders for more drinks.

CHAPTER 45

Outside the yard, the bachelors' eve party was picking up steam. People were streaming in. This is the last day of bachelorhood and spinsterhood for Ike and Nneka. Tomorrow they would wed in the Church. Everything was moving smoothly.

As the dusk gathered, building lights glittered like heavenly stars afar off. Oliaku watched the scenario from the balcony. She was fascinated by the array of lights doting residential houses. She had never seen a thing like that. With all the niceties in the city, she concluded that city dwellers were enjoying life more abundantly than those in the rural areas. She wondered why everyone else should not converge at the city. Why should some people live in the village, while others live in the cities enjoying the easy life?

Another attraction was the music coming from down stairs. It added grace to Oliaku's evening. She had never listened to highlife music. The high powered speaker blasted tunes by local artists like Bobby Benson, Victor

Olaya, Eddy Okonta, Israel Nwoba, Dan Njemanze, and a host of musicians of those days. The reverberating bass of the music seemed to shake the building causing pulsating and scary feelings in Oliaku. She held tight unto the rails of the balcony afraid that the resonating sound of music might cause the building to collapse. She ran inside and complained to Emeka who laughed and reassured her.

The party was in full swing now. People streamed in and out, eating and drinking. Ike's friends and relatives stopped by to drop off presents, so did Nneka's friends. Those who could not stay throughout the night simply took a few drinks and left, while others, especially the young folks, stayed partying.

At the center of the gathering, young men and women drank and danced. The DJ dished out the music that the people wanted, and everybody was drinking and dancing merrily. Booze and food were plenty. Ike was well off. People ate, drank, and danced.

The atmosphere was filled with blithe and merriment. Oliaku was all eyes. She couldn't believe all she was seeing tonight. No wonder people talk a lot about township life, she thought as she watched the dancers. This is what goes on everyday in the townships - happiness, merry-making, entertainment, and enjoyment. There is no farming here, no fishing, no hunting, and no hard work. Yet people eat everyday. There's easy life here. I wish I could come here to live.

A combination of red, blue, yellow, and green light hung in spherical form above. This array of lighting generated a glamorous illumination that shone resplendently on the guests below. Chairs were arranged in a circular form. Boys and girls danced in the middle of the circle, a small group at a time. Three giant loudspeakers stood at each corner at the background. The scene was orderly and magnificent.

Bachelors' eve usually lasted into the early hours of the morning, and at daybreak, the bride and the bridegroom would head to the altar.

At eleven o'clock the chairman of the occasion, Mr. Cyril Amakom, made a special announcement,

"Ladies and gentlemen, you will agree with me that in the history of bachelors' eve, there has never been any celebration as spectacular as this one. It is outstanding. It is exceptional. Food and drinks are surplus. The music is fantastic. I'm highly impressed, and I believe everybody is overwhelmed with the splendid and admirable enjoyment going on here. But there is one thing that is still missing. Ikechukwu Anierobi and Nneka Akigwe must come here to bid us farewell because in a couple of hours they will leave bachelorhood and spinsterhood to advance into another phase of their lives."

By this statement, Mr. Amakom was inviting Ikechukwu and Nneka to come out and dance. That was the custom and the climax of the celebration.

Ike was upstairs putting things together for tomorrow, but Nneka was downstairs watching the dancers. She was enjoying herself.

During a bachelors' eve, comic stories and anecdotes, jokes and humours were unleashed at the candidates. Comedians cause people to laugh off their ribs. Bachelors and spinsters tease the hosts for the last time. The jokes and humours amused Nneka and she was laughing her ribs off. She was surrounded by her friends.

After Mr. Amakom had spoken, a man with wobbling gait took the microphone, "Someone should go upstairs to fetch Ikechukwu and Nneka. We need them to come and teach us how to dance."

The audience laughed and chorused, "Yes! Yes! Yes! They should come and dance."

He was still speaking when Ike and Nneka entered the foreground. Ovation greeted them as Ike led his wife into the center and began to dance. The people hailed and clapped their hands. With every move the couple made, the crowd yelled and shouted praises.

Shortly after, Monica, who was to be Nneka's chief bridesmaid, joined them in the circle. Nneka had earlier intimated Monica to join her during their dance to save her from the embarrassment of her clumsy style. The crowd was thrilled.

As the deafening loudspeakers blared into the coolness of the night, people were enraptured in their enjoyment. They shouted acclamation and bravados to the dancers. They clapped hands and raised their fists for every move the couple made.

Suddenly, in the midst of the ecstasy and merriment, two masked men burst into the scene from nowhere and began shooting at the dancers.

Panic!

There was confusion and pandemonium in the crowd, followed by a mad stampede and rush. Chaos! People ran for their lives screaming and crying. The music stopped abruptly. People toppled over one another as they tried to escape; chairs and tables were knocked over; basins of food were pushed down; cartons of drinks spilled over; glasses shattered; electric stands and music apparatuses were knocked down. A hazy scene of bestial chaos prevailed. The showground was deserted in a matter of seconds.

The two masked men had gunned down Ike, Nneka, and Monica and vanished. Nobody knew who the gunmen were nor where they came from. The victims lay on the ground bleeding and crying for help. It was a startling confusion. The violent anarchy dazed everyone.

Nobody came forward to help the wounded for fear the shooting might continue. Many people who attended the event had fled.

Not quite long thereafter, the atmosphere quietened. An uneasy calm hung in the air. Some men began to crawl out of their hiding. One by one, people emerged stunned. They began to attend to the wounded. In fear and bewilderment, they stared at one another seeking an answer to the puzzle that had just taken place.

"What's the meaning of all this?" one man asked.

"Never in the history of our land has such a tragic incident taken place," another man said.

Women were crying. People were shocked and confused, tongues were tied, and faces were horror-stricken. They shook their heads in perplexity.

"Let's take these people to the hospital," Mr. Amakom appealed to the men.

"Yes, let's rush them to the hospital before they all bleed to death," said another man.

"No more fear men," said a young man. "Let's do some work here. The vagabonds can come back and shoot all of us, who cares. Let's save the wounded people. This is a task for us, we must save these lives. Come out of your hiding places."

With shaking and trembling limbs, the men rallied round and set to work.

Quickly, Ike, Nneka, and Monica were lifted into a waiting car. They were rushed to the Hospital. Guests who sustained bullet wounds were also taken to the hospital. Unfortunately Nneka did not make it to the hospital. Monica made it to the hospital but gave up on the operating table.

Ike remained unconscious and on the critical list. He had lost a lot of blood. He received many bullet wounds at various parts of his body. Two shots were fatal. One shot went through his left shoulder, exactly on the spot where the Nzom fishermen goaded his shoulder with a spear. The other shot pierced his neck vertebra, narrowly missing his spinal cord column.

CHAPTER 46

The following day the news about the catastrophic incident spread all over the town. The morning newspapers carried stories of a couple murdered at their bachelors' eve. The story had spread throughout the country.

Onitsha was shaken after the dastard shooting. Rumours began to circulate regarding the origin of the attack. Different interpretations were given to it. Some people said it was the work of a rival suitor; some said it was armed robbers looking for money; others said someone might be settling an old score.

Detectives at Onitsha went into action. Secret agents were dispatched to all corners of the city to sniff out the mystery surrounding the attack on the new Managing Director of the Peoples Bank and his bride. The headquarters of the Peoples Bank in Lagos despatched representatives to Onitsha to assist in the investigation.

Following a tipoff, detectives raided a criminal hideout at Nkisi and rounded up some men of the underworld. Further investigations by the Police CID, revealed that

Ikechukwu Anierobi, the Managing Director of the Peoples Bank, was the prime target of the brutal attack. It was also discovered that Alfred Anierobi, his cousin, was linked to the homicide. He was arrested and put behind bars while Police investigations continued.

Doctors and nurses at the Iyienu Hospital battled relentlessly to save Ike's life. Five days after his admission to the hospital, he regained consciousness. He had profuse internal bleeding. The multiple gun-shots had opened up major blood vessels in his body. The doctors kept him on continuous blood transfusion for four days. No one believed that Ike would survive, but on the fifth day, they announced that he was going to make it.

"This man is lucky," said doctor Peter Nwata to his nurses during one of their ward-rounds. "I've never seen such a lucky man."

"You're right doctor," agreed nurse Ezedike, "Mr. Anierobi is simply lucky. I thought he was going to die. He lost all the blood in his system."

"Correct, but his savior was that no major organ was damaged," Dr. Nwata explained. "The bullets did not touch the heart, liver, lungs, etc. His spinal cord missed a bullet by a thread. He is a very lucky man."

Ike was kept in the V.I.P Ward in room 5. Not all visitors were allowed in the V.I.P. section. Ministers, Permanent Secretaries, doctors, and some wealthy personalities, were the class of citizens kept in the VIP Ward. Only a few close relatives were permitted to enter that section.

Ike received special attention from the doctors and nurses. The nurses were at his bedside twenty-four hours monitoring his prognosis. All hands were on deck to ensure this man's survival.

The moment Ike regained consciousness, he said: "Where's my sweetheart?"

That question presented a puzzle to Nurse Agnes Okugo who was doing the *vital signs* when Ike spoke for the first time. From her training, Nurse Okugo knew she must not divulge any news to a patient who was in a critical or life-threatening condition. Besides, the Nursing Sister, Mrs. Mary Acho, had warned her nurses not to reveal Nneka's death to Ike should he demand to know about his wife. The head nurse didn't want to worsen his condition by untimely disclosure.

In response to Ike's question, therefore, the nurse lied. She told Ike that Nneka was in the female Ward.

Nurse Okugo was still speaking when Sister Acho opened the door and walked in. She was glad when she heard Ike talking. "Yes, your wife is in the female Ward," said Sister Acho, "and she is making progress.

Ike did not know that his beloved bride had been buried on Sunday which would've been their wedding day. Nneka's death was hidden from him. Sister Acho had given instructions to everybody to stick to this falsehood until Ike attained a good level of recovery.

Everybody complied with this instruction, but Dr. Eric Jones, an American Youth Copper who was working at the hospital, opposed the idea.

"Tell him the damn truth," Dr. Jones said, sitting at the edge of Sister Acho's table. "The sooner he knew about the loss, the better for him."

"No," Sister Acho disagreed. "I don't think it's a good idea to tell this patient about the death of his bride at this time. When he gains enough strength to deal with the shock, we'll let him know. Not now."

Doctor Jones wasn't satisfied with that answer. He plunged into an argument with the nursing Sister. "In my country, this is the function of Social Workers," he explained. "A Social Worker takes the matter up with the patient. He or she would work with the patient gradually until the patient accepts the loss. I don't think it is proper to postpone the grieving process. It's unprofessional to hide such vital information from the patient because he has the right to know what happened to his wife. *Men,* that's how it's done in America".

"I see. But this is Nigeria," Sister Acho declared. "We are in Nigeria, not in America. In our own setting such a traumatic blow is handled very carefully, or else you create more problems. You don't break sad news to a victim with despatch. We have a way of imparting traumatic information to victims, especially weak and fragile patients, to minimize the degree of shock. This is traditional to us, it is not written in medical books. Unless you want to cause another problem, the best approach is to reduce the impact of shock, because at this critical point, the patient's emotional capacity and disposition are on edge and may not withstand such a shocking revelation."

Dr. Jones wasn't impressed. "I think Mr. Anierobi gonna take offense when he discovers that his wife's death was deliberately hidden from him. I bet you, he's gonna feel more offended than bereaved."

"He would not," said the nursing Sister. "Mr. Anierobi is part of this culture. He knows we don't break sad news in that manner. We value human feelings. Africans are humane. We value and respect human feelings..."

"Who doesn't?" interjected Dr. Jones, both hands in his overall.

"You do, but not the way Africans do it. It's improper in our own setting to announce a horrible news to such a feeble mind like you do in the Western world. I know that in your own setting, you break sad news to the bereaved and you sit back to watch them reel in pain. And then you offer them tissue paper to wipe their tears. I heard about a young student who was just about to begin her final exam, when someone walked into the hall and whispered to her that her mother had just died in a ghastly motor accident. What do you expect that girl to write in the exam? We don't do that here, we can postpone that ugly news. In Africa, we have feelings for others, what touches one touches the other; what pains one pains the other; and what affects one affects the other. We have a way of sharing grief. We have a way of cushioning shocks or rendering support to enable a victim to absorb trauma with less of a crush. Some cultures don't give a damn. Some cultures don't grieve with the aggrieved; some don't empathize with all their hearts. Good for them."

Sister Acho was charged over what has escalated into an argument between the American Youth Corper and herself. The nurses were listening to the discussion. They knew that Sister Acho would not give in. They respected her and her vast knowledge of nursing administration and human psychology. Hands crossed behind her back, the chief nurse went on:

"I'm speaking from experience, Dr. Jones. I've had similar cases in the past. For example, a couple was involved in a fatal motor accident. The man died, but the wife survived with critical injuries. When the young lady regained consciousness in her hospital bed, she asked about her husband?' A naive nursing assistant blabbed the news right away. The woman slumped back into coma. She never woke up. Perhaps the poor woman would've survived if the information was delayed. Perhaps she would've been alive today if the nurses had allowed her to regain enough strength, physically and emotionally, before the sad news."

All the nurses and doctors in the office pitched camp with Sister Acho on her views. Dr. Jones did not understand, or perhaps, he did not want to understand. He stuck to his views, albeit he complied with Sister Acho's instructions that nobody should disclose to Ike that Nneka was dead.

Several times Ike wrote a short note to Nneka whom he believed was recovering in Ward 4. In the notes sent through the nurses, he wished Nneka speedy recovery. Little did he know that Nneka was lying in the grave at Ifite. One of Ike's letters read:

"Oh darling, I'm glad you're alive. You must be in pain. Take heart Nne. They told me you're making some progress. Good! Keep your spirit up. I learnt you sustained more injuries

than I did. Oh, I wish I were there to hold you in my arms. I can imagine your aches and pains. I wish I could take the pain away. Have courage my love, it's just a question of time and everything will be fine and we shall proceed to the altar. The planned wedding must take place. I must give you a wonderful wedding when we leave the hospital - a wedding ever witnessed anywhere in the world. Thank God we survived. I wish you a speedy recovery my love. I can't wait to see you. My heart is aching for you, and my eyes are itching to see you. I'm still very weak, but as soon as I can move, I will come to see you."

> *Yours forever,*
> *Ike A.*

Some nurses cried when they read the letters Ike wrote to his wife. Of course Ike never got a reply from Nneka. The nurses told him that they read the letters to her and that she was still unable to write. One day, they faked a reply and gave to Ike, implying that his wife dictated the information. Ike read it and felt better.

CHAPTER 47

One afternoon Sister Acho, nurse Amaka Ezedike, nurse Immaculata Okonkwo, and nurse Nkechi Onovo, sat around Ike's bed chatting with him as they often did. However the purpose of today's meeting was different. Sister Acho, in her professional assessment, believed that the time was ripe to disclose to Ike about his wife's death. The nursing sister believed that Mr. Anierobi was now strong enough to handle the sad news.

Ike could eat by himself now, instead of being fed. He could also chat with the nurses and even crack little jokes. Initially food was ingested into his stomach via a tube. After he had improved, the tube was removed and the nurses fed him because his hands were riddled with bullets. His left shoulder was shattered, and his right elbow was broken. Also the bullet that pierced his vertebrae grazed the delicate spinal tissue. This caused occasional nervous twitches, spasms, and numbness. Only Heavens knew how Ike survived. Even the doctors and nurses were surprised at his recovery.

As the nurses chatted quietly and mirthlessly around Ike's bed, Sister Acho said, "Mr. Anierobi, let me ask you a question."

"Yes," Ike replied turning his head painstakingly. He grimaced. His wounds were hurting. The nurses were silent with their eyes fixed on Sister Acho. They knew why they were there. They knew what was coming. The bombshell would soon be dropped. Sister Acho was experienced in handling such issues. She had done it umpteen times.

"How do you describe a man who has the quality of endurance, and is able to absorb the shock of a tragic incident?" Sister Acho asked Ike, just pretending to raise a topic of conversation. Her facial appearance was normal and did not betray the contents of her heart. The nurses were not in a jovial mood as they used to be. Their faces looked tense and gloomy, almost giving away the secret. Nurse Ezedike in particular wore a dizzy and desolate look.

"What do you mean Sister?" Ike asked with a faint smile, a little confused.

"When something happens, something that is painful and tragic, I don't care what it is, it could be a motor accident, it could be death, it could be a serious injury, it could be a loss or anything, the affected person or persons take the matter with courage and fortitude as if nothing had happened. How do you qualify men and women who possess such qualities?"

Ike stared at the pole that held his drip. "If I understand your question clearly," he said with difficulty, "people usually say that the individual has courage and power of endurance. In other words, it is said that the individual has *the heart of a man*."

"Excellent!" Sister Acho acclaimed. "That was a perfect answer. That's what you are, and that's exactly what I expect you to continue to be throughout this ordeal. You have indeed come a long way. You have endured a lot.

The Sister crossed her legs and studied Ike's mood to determine how prepared he was to receive the bitter pill. The three nurses were watching, hands across their chests, a good indication that something was wrong. Nobody was smiling as usual. Their faces wore hazy looks.

"What is life?" The Sister asked again, and she supplied the answer. "Nothing but a shadow - a temporal realm where nothing holds and where mankind is simply on transit. Since the beginning of time, many strange and eerie things have happened to humanity and continue to happen. It is said that nothing is new under the sun.

Ike was listening very attentively. In his opinion, the Sister's sermon was only a consolation for what had happened to him and his wife. Little did he know that the therapy was a forerunner of a shocking revelation. The preaching was designed to cushion the effect of what was coming.

"We die but once," Sister Acho continued. "And all of us are destined to die. A major puzzle is, no one knows when death shall come. When we lose a very dear one, our hearts bleed, our spirits sag. We feel powerless and despondent. Sometimes we're depressed to the point of wanting to quit life.

Ike remained quiet listening to the Senior Nurse. As the lecture progressed, he began to wonder where the

Sister was going with all this. Albeit, he remained attentive digesting the comforting message from the kind lady.

"I look at you as a brave man with courageous personality. From your life history, you are someone who has gone through difficult experiences. You possess the spirit of endurance, and the heart to absorb a shock. That's what you described at the beginning as 'having the heart of a man'. I believe you have the heart of a man."

No one spoke except the Senior Nurse. The nurses were quiet. They remained glued to their seats. The situation was beginning to look explosive. The nurses knew the zero hour had come. They knew that Sister Acho, in her style, would first gloat over the precincts before wading into the core of the substance.

Ike seemed to read meaning into the nurses' mood. No smiles, no jokes, no teasing. The cheerfulness they carried on their faces at all times was missing. In its place, solemnity and void. They made no contributions to what the Sister was saying. They simply stared at the Managing Director with downcast looks.

In normal circumstances, they would be cackling, giggling, and laughing. They would be teasing their patient. Nurse Okonkwo would say,

"Mr. Anierobi, let's do a marathon race."

Nurse Ezedike would say,

"Mr. Anierobi, I need a loan from your bank."

And nurse Nkechi Onovo would say, "Mr. Anierobi, banks pay very well, I will resign and work for you."

They would all be joking and laughing. But today there was no joke and no laughter. Their mood and comportment were grave and suspicious. The atmosphere itself was tense. The door was locked. No nurse came in to deliver food, medication, or anything. Even the three-hourly injection was compromised for this important talk, so was the routine vital sign check.

At this juncture, Ike was a little confused. He felt within himself that this *sermon on the mountain* was stretching into something indiscernible. It sounded like a consolation treatise. Has anything happened? he wondered within himself. His heart began to pump faster. He darted his eyes at the three nurses in quick succession. He knew they had never been so quiet and morose, and that something might be wrong.

"Is everything okay?" Ike asked and looked at Sister Acho, and then at the nurses.

There was silence. No one responded to that question. He became worried and anxious.

"Is everything all right?" Ike asked again.

He looked helplessly at each of them in turn. He became confused. He had the premonition that all was not well.

Instead of saying something, the nurses looked on. Their silence was ominous. In the normal circumstances, their response would be: Oh yes, everything is fine. Not even the senior nurse said anything.

Ike, therefore, suspected that something must be wrong because nobody was speaking. "Can someone tell me what is happening please? Is anything wrong?" he asked, again and again. "Everybody is quiet, is anything wrong ladies?"

"Yes." Sister Acho replied at last and rose on her feet. She took a step forward and placed a hand on Ike's chest and spoke in a very calm, sober, and calculated voice, "Be a man now."

"What happened?" Ike demanded quickly, his eyes wide open and his voice was shaky.

He raised his head and tried to come to a sitting position.

"We shall tell you," said Sister Acho.

"Is Nneka okay?" Ike broke out immediately.

Again silence. No one spoke. They just stared.

"You've got to tell me what has happened," he demanded in a cracked and trembling voice.

He now knew that something had happened.

"Why don't you tell me what has happened. Is anything wrong?"

"Yes," Sister Acho replied. "Something is wrong. And we know that you can handle it with the heart of a man."

"What is it? What happened? Is Nneka okay? Is she dead?"

"Yes," replied Sister Acho.

"Oh my soul!" Ike bemoaned in a loud voice and slumped backwards. "Ohooooo! Ohooooo! Good gracious! Ohooooo! Ohooooo - no! no! no! Ohooooo! Nne, Nne, Nneka m, Ohooooooooo!"

The nurses watched as he cried and sobbed. They also cried.

"Your wife died on that bachelors' eve, "Sister Acho said." She died on her way to the hospital. She never made it to the hospital. The other lady who was dancing with her died on the operating table. All of you were riddled with bullets. Only you survived."

Sister Acho paused for a minute. Ike cried bitterly with deep emotion. He grated his teeth and waved his head repeatedly.

"We're sorry we couldn't disclose the sad news before now. We were concerned about your health. We wanted you to be emotionally prepared to accept the loss."

The door was locked all the while. Nobody was in the room except the four nurses. But immediately after the news was broken, nurse Immaculata Okonkwo who was still crying, rose and opened the door. Nurse Ngbako led three men and two women into the room. Two of them were Ike's relatives, the other man was Ike's best friend, Mr. Okezie, who would've been the best man in the ill-fated wedding. The women were their wives.

Sister Acho had arranged for these people to stand by when the death of Ike's wife would be revealed to him so they would render support.

At this point, the nurses returned to their work wiping their eyes. Ike's friends and relatives surrounded his bed and consoled him.

CHAPTER 48

Two months had passed since Ike's admission to the hospital. He had made tremendous progress. Psychologically, he was still devastated about Nneka's death. He was mentally and emotionally shattered and heart-broken. He felt that life without Nneka was meaningless. He was torn apart to learn that the girl he was getting ready to take to the altar after recovery had since been buried. Nothing was more devastating.

"So I won't see Nneka any more in my life?" he said. "So my heart-desire is gone forever? Is it true that my Nne is dead? What is life without Nneka? Ohooooo! Life is cruel. Life is useless. Life is baseless."

Ike wondered if he was going to recover from this tragedy. Nevertheless, gradually he began to pull out of the doldrums. He had no choice than to hold fast unto life. His pains had reduced considerably, and his arms and neck were out of the cast. He could now sit up on a chair, go to the bathroom, walk around, and even do some writing. He had regained significant strength and energy to push on with what remained of his life. The doctors had indicated he'd be discharged the following week to continue his recovery at home.

With the help of the doctors, nurses, friends and relatives, Ike was healing, both physically and emotionally. The nurses and doctors at the Iyienu hospital were very helpful. But there was one particular nurse who took special interest in attending to Ike since his arrival in the hospital. She was nurse Mgbako.

Nurse Mgbako was always at Ike's bedside. She worked very assiduously and devotedly for this man. Nurse Mgbako did more than every other nurse in caring for Ike. Apart from the routine hospital duties, nurse Mgbako ran errands for Ike. She went to the stores to buy his little needs; she went to the Post Office; she took messages to his family and to his office. Ike was very appreciative of nurse Mgbako's assistance, especially for the personal attention she gave him. He became so close to her and would always send her on errands.

One day before he left the hospital, a ten-year-old boy, well dressed and cute, visited him and stood at his bedside smiling. Ike smiled and greeted the boy, "Young man, how are you?"

"Fine Sir, thank you."

"Did you come to visit me?" Ike asked him cheerfully.

"Yes Sir, and also to introduce myself to you."

Ike assumed he was the child of one of his friends who occasionally stopped by to see him. But he was surprised because children did not stray into the VIP rooms unless in the company of an adult.

As the boy was speaking, the door opened and nurse Mgbako walked in and put a hand on the boy's shoulder.

"I have a visitor," Ike announced to nurse Mgbako in a lighter mood. "What's your name, my friend?" Ike asked the boy.

"My name is Ikechukwu," the boy replied, shyly.

"Oh, my namesake, right?"

"Right, but more than your namesake," nurse Mgbako replied before the boy could respond.

Ike did not understand.

"Did you say more than my namesake?"

"Yes," nurse Mgbako replied. "He is more than your namesake."

"Why? What do you mean?" Ike laughed, a little puzzled.

Instead of explaining herself and what she meant by, 'he's more than your namesake,' nurse Mgbako remained silent trying desperately to control her tears.

Ike was confused. What's the meaning of this? he thought.

Amidst sobs she told Ike that she was Angela, his first girl friend at No. 3 Ekwulobia Street Onitsha. "This boy is that pregnancy," Angela disclosed and burst out crying.

As soon as nurse Mgbako mentioned her name, Ike recognized Angela. He was speechless, his former girlfriend many years ago.

All along, since nurse Ngbako was assisting him in the hospital, Ike never recognized her. The nurse did not reveal her identity. He stared at Angela speechless. The true picture of the girl reappeared vividly in his memory.

He recapitulated the whole event between him and Angela years back. He staggered unto his feet. Overwhelmed with joy, he embraced mother and child saying, "Is this Angela, my first love? Is this my child? Is he that pregnancy? Is this you, Angie? Is this my own son, and my Angie? I can't believe this. Heavens come down!"

READER'S COMMENTS

1. *The Apprentice Boy is a masterpiece art which portrays the tradition of the Igbo people of Nigeria and the bravery of a young man. Dr. Luke Okoli takes great style and form in crafting this unique piece of art. It is beautiful from the first line.*
   Kent Anderson, Australia.

2. *This is a classical novel and an engaging story. Luke Okoli skillfully weaves fiction into reality. Michael Major Fernandez – Mexico.*

3. *A great novel by an African author. Its colorful character will remain with the reader for a long time. – Bruce Mangrum, USA.*

4. *The Apprentice Boy offers a lot about African tradition and African way of life. Ike is presented in a livid and exemplary fashion – B. Cochran, UK*

5. *I could hardly put down The Apprentice Boy till the end. It's the best contemporary African novel I have read. I can't wait for Part II Josiah Annan, Ghana.*